The Memoir of a Flash Dancer

A novel by

Anastasia Parakhnevich

1

The Memoir of a Flash Dancer: a novel

ISBN: 979-8-99307793-2

Published by A.Parakhnevich

The Memoir of a Flash Dancer

Prologue

I saw her in pieces.

I saw her Sun.

A flicker in ruin,

Too bright to outrun.

When life wrote its theses,

In smoke and in bone,

She carved out my silence

And died on a throne.

Chapter 1: Welcome to New York

The bus smelled like old dreams and fast food. Charlotte sat with her forehead pressed against the cold window, watching the skyline rise in the distance like a promise or a threat. She hadn't slept in twenty-four hours. Her phone was dead. Her duffel bag held everything she owned that mattered: a pair of platform heels, a half-used bottle of perfume, and an envelope with exactly $284.

New York didn't care.

She tried not to overthink it. The longer she stared at the city, the more it seemed to stare back like it already knew all her secrets. Like it could smell her fear.
She stepped off the bus into a slap of cold spring air, the kind that still smelled like leftover winter. The city was loud, aggressive, a blur of horns and voices and feet that never stopped moving. She tugged her denim jacket tighter and tried to look like she belonged.

Lilly was late. Of course she was.
Charlotte stood there on the corner of 42nd and hopeless, watching taxis blur past in streaks of yellow. The wind cut through her clothes. A thousand strangers brushed by, none of them

offering a second glance. She lit a cigarette she didn't want and waited.

Twenty minutes later, a black Altima rolled up, bass thumping. The passenger window rolled down, and a familiar voice called, "Get in, small-town Barbie."
Lilly looked exactly like she did on Instagram - curled lashes, leather jacket, glossy lips. Only in real life, she had that tired tension around the eyes that pictures never showed.

"You made it," she said as Charlotte slid in. "Welcome to hell."
Charlotte laughed, more out of nerves than humor. "You're late."
"Get used to it. Everything in this city runs on stripper time."
They drove in silence for a while. Charlotte stared out at the blur of buildings, graffiti-covered walls, fire escapes, and street vendors. Everything looked worn and alive, like it had survived something.
"You nervous?" Lilly asked, glancing over.
"I'm terrified."
"Good. Means you're not stupid."

Lilly's apartment was on the third floor of a walk-up in Queens. The hallway smelled like curry and bleach. The inside was small but surprisingly homey - candles burning low, Christmas lights strung across the ceiling, makeup and fake lashes scattered on the coffee table. A tiny black cat blinked at Charlotte from the arm of the couch.

"You can sleep here," Lilly said, motioning to a stack of folded blankets.
Charlotte dropped her duffel. "Thanks for letting me crash."
"Don't thank me yet. Rent's due in five days. You're gonna be hustling quick."
Charlotte nodded. She didn't come to New York to relax.
"So…" she began, hesitating. "How does it work?"
Lilly pulled a tiny black dress from her closet - more suggestion than fabric and tossed it to her.
"We leave in an hour. You're wearing this."
Charlotte held it up between two fingers. "There's nothing here."
"That's the point." Lilly grinned. "You'll do fine. You've got the face of a saint and legs for sin. Men are gonna lose their minds."
"I've never really danced," Charlotte admitted, lowering her voice.

"You'll figure it out. They don't come for technique. They come for the fantasy."
Charlotte went quiet. In her head, she heard her mother's voice. Her grandmother's. All the women back home who folded laundry, said

prayers, and never once dared to dream of velvet stages and champagne rooms.

But she hadn't come all this way to be a good girl.
The club looked like something from a movie.
It was housed in an old Beaux-Arts building nestled between a high-end tailor and a luxury watch shop in Midtown. An ornate archway framed the entrance, carved with floral patterns and gargoyles that watched from above like stone angels. There was no sign, no flashy lights. Just a sleek brass plaque that read VIP Members Only and a velvet rope guarded by a man in a tailored black coat.
Lilly gave him a nod. He buzzed them in without a word.
Charlotte stepped into another world.
The foyer was dimly lit, bathed in soft amber light that reflected off gold-framed mirrors. The air was perfumed and warm, carrying notes of vanilla, rose, and something faintly spicy luxury bottled and sprayed with intention. Thick red velvet drapes lined the walls, and polished marble floors stretched out beneath her heels.
Every detail whispered exclusivity. Mystery. Money.
She followed Lilly down a hallway that pulsed with music. The bass was low, seductive. The walls seemed to breathe with it.

"This place is insane," Charlotte whispered.
Lilly smirked. "You haven't seen anything yet."
They stepped into the main room, and Charlotte's breath caught.

The space opened up like a dream - vaulted ceilings, chandeliers dripping with crystals, sleek leather booths tucked in shadowed corners. The stage was long, wide, glowing with light and surrounded by a ring of plush armchairs where suited men leaned back like kings.

A dancer twirled on the pole, her body glistening, her hair like liquid gold under the lights. Her heels caught the light as she arched her back and dropped into a split that made a few nearby customers audibly exhale.

Charlotte couldn't look away. It was mesmerizing. Powerful. Beautiful in a way that wasn't soft, but fierce.

"C'mon," Lilly nudged. "Let's get you to the dressing room."

They pushed through a side hallway and entered the backstage area. It was chaos wrapped in glitter.

The dressing room buzzed with the sound of curling irons, pop music, laughter, arguments, and the rustling of lingerie. Girls of every shape and color were squeezed into thongs, adjusting bras, painting lips, brushing out hair. It smelled like body spray, sweat, and hot tools.

"Ladies," Lilly called, "fresh meat!"

Heads turned. Some smiled. Others barely looked.

"That's Aliana," Lilly whispered, pointing toward a curvy girl with bronze skin and warm eyes who gave Charlotte a wave. "She's solid. Has your back. Trust her."

"And that?" Charlotte asked, nodding toward a tall blonde with sculpted cheekbones and an icy stare.

"Valery. Thinks she's the queen. Keep your distance unless you like drama."

A woman appeared: petite, sharp-eyed, clipboard in hand.

"Name?"

Charlotte blinked. "Uh… Charlotte."

The woman squinted at her. "Too plain. Stage name?"

Charlotte hesitated.

"She's Starr," Lilly said before she could answer.

"Fine. Booth three. DJ calls your name, you hit the stage. Don't trip."

As Starr peeled off her jacket and stepped into the borrowed dress, something shifted. Her reflection in the mirror shimmered into someone else. Her lips were red now. Her lashes long. Her hair teased high and wild. She looked dangerous. She looked like a secret.

She didn't feel like Charlotte anymore.

A little while later, Lilly led her through the back hallways and into the main room for her first walk-through. They moved past the bar, where a hot blonde bartender gave them a lazy nod. Past the DJ booth, where a man in a velvet blazer adjusted sliders on the soundboard. Past the champagne room doors, guarded by two thick-necked men in suits.

Near the end of the bar, a tall man sat alone in a leather booth. He was broad-shouldered, salt-and-pepper hair, expensive watch. He didn't look up when they passed, but Lilly leaned in and whispered, "That's Steve. The owner."

Charlotte shivered. Something about him felt cold, even from a distance.

And next to the DJ booth, lounging like he owned the place, was a boy who couldn't have been more than twenty-three. He was wearing a black tee, gold chain, eyes scanning the floor like a predator picking his moment. He noticed them. Smiled at Starr.

"That's his son Dylan," Lilly muttered. "Watch out for him."

Starr looked back at him just for a second too long.

And he looked right back.

She was nervous. Her stomach twisted. Her hands shook. But when the DJ called her name: "Next on stage, give it up for Starr" - she walked.

The lights hit her. The music swelled. The floor felt like lava beneath her feet.

She wrapped her hands around the pole, exhaled, and started to move.

She didn't know what she was doing. But no one else seemed to notice. The men leaned forward. The lights made her glow. For three minutes, she wasn't afraid. She wasn't Charlotte.

She was a star.

Chapter 2: Baptism by Fire

The stage lights faded behind her, but their afterglow still burned in her veins. Her skin felt electric, buzzing with adrenaline, shame, and something close to hunger. She didn't know if she should cry or laugh. Maybe both.
No one had booed. No one had thrown a drink. Instead, they watched her with silent, greedy eyes and some of them even clapped.
Not because she was good. But because she was new.
Lilly met her at the edge of the hallway, cigarette dangling from her lips, thick eyeliner smudged like war paint. "You didn't die. That's a win."
Starr managed a smile, but her fingers trembled. Her skin felt foreign tight, hot, exposed. "That was... something."
Lilly handed her a shot of something bright and poisonous. "You'll learn to love it. Or at least live with it."
She swallowed it fast, let it burn down her throat like a reminder: she'd chosen this. Every second from here on out was her responsibility.
"Now," Lilly said, cracking her neck, "time to learn how to hustle."

The floor was full now. The real show started after midnight.

The club glowed like a jewel box purple neon licking the edges of polished floors, crystal chandeliers catching light like fire. Booths were filled with men in expensive suits, plastic watches, and wide eyes. There was a rhythm to the chaos: the beat of bass, the clink of glass, the whispered negotiations behind curtains.

Starr moved through it like a ghost, guided by Lilly.

"This is where you make your money," Lilly whispered, her voice low and sharp. "The stage gets their attention. But the floor? That's where you drain their wallets."

They stopped near a table. A man in his forties with too much cologne and too little self-awareness was already looking at Starr like she was dessert. Lilly gave her a nudge.

"Rule one," she said, "walk like you've already been paid."

Starr stepped forward. Her heart pounded against her ribs like a trapped animal, but she smiled. Sat down. Let her eyes do the work.

"New girl?" the man asked, sipping his scotch.

"First night," she said.

He grinned, eyes sliding down her body. "Well then. Let's celebrate."

His hand found her thigh. She didn't flinch. She didn't lean into it either. Just held the smile like armor. Fake it, she told herself. Fake it till you forget what's real.

The man shoved two bills into her bra without looking at them. She didn't either.

"You're going to do well," he said. "You've got that 'sad but hopeful' look. Men love that."

She didn't reply. Just adjusted her bra and moved on.

Backstage smelled like sweat, hair spray, and secrets.

Starr collapsed onto a bench; heels tossed aside. Her toes were swollen, her calves aching. She was sticky with stage lights and strange hands.

She counted her tips with trembling fingers. $387. In three hours.

Her chest tightened. Not with fear. With possibility.

Aliana slid next to her, already halfway through a banana and still in full lashes. "Not bad, rookie."

"Everything hurts," Starr muttered.

"Get used to it. Pain is part of the package."

"Do you ever... forget who you are in here?"

Aliana took a long look at her. "I remember who I was before this. And I remember how much that girl suffered. So no, I don't forget. I just don't miss her."

Starr stared down at the stack of bills in her lap. They didn't feel real. Neither did she.

"Stick with me," Aliana said. "I'll show you how to survive."

Starr smiled, and for a moment, it didn't feel fake. Then Valery walked by.

Blonde. Built like a lingerie model with an attitude to match. She paused at the mirror, reapplied her lipstick, and cast a sideways glance.

"She won't last a month," Valery said casually, and left.

Aliana rolled her eyes. "Ignore her. She thinks being cold makes her strong."

Starr swallowed. "Is she wrong?"

Aliana's voice was soft. "Not always."

She met Rob after her fourth dance.

He found her in the hallway, her knees still wobbling, eyeliner smeared.

"You're Starr?" he asked.

She nodded.

"You did alright. Better than some."

His voice was calm, kind. It didn't match the chaos.

"I don't really know what I'm doing," she admitted.

"You'll learn. This place will teach you everything, just not gently."

There was something in his eyes. Something heavy. Like he'd seen too many girls like her come and go.

"You seem like a good kid," he said. "Don't get lost in it."

She wanted to ask what "it" meant, but she already knew.

She saw Dylan that same night.

He was leaning against the bar, phone in one hand, whiskey in the other. Young, polished, effortlessly arrogant. His eyes found hers like he'd been waiting.

"Starr," he said, smiling like the devil wore cologne.

"You know my name?"

"I make it my business."

She stopped walking.

He took her in slowly eyes roaming, resting. He didn't hide it. Didn't rush it. "You don't belong here."

She laughed under her breath. "Neither do you."

"I was born here."

"Then maybe that's worse."

He stepped closer. She didn't back away.

"You're different," he said. "Most of them want something. I can't figure out what you want yet."

"Maybe that's the point."

He grinned. "Clever. I like that."

He brushed a stray strand of hair from her shoulder, fingers just grazing her skin. A spark lit in her stomach - danger, desire, or both.

"Don't fall for the fantasy, Starr," he whispered. "This place eats good girls alive."

"Then I guess I'm in the right place," she said, and walked away.

But her pulse stayed with him.

By week's end, she was bruised, richer, and more confused than ever.

She danced in the champagne room for a man who didn't touch her, just stared at her like she was a poem he couldn't finish. He paid her four hundred dollars and said she reminded him of someone he used to love.

She took the money. She didn't ask questions.

Back in the dressing room, Valery muttered something about "fast risers" and "easy money."

Starr didn't respond. She just stuffed the bills into her bag and reapplied her lipstick.

She was learning.

To keep quiet. To watch. To disappear when necessary and shine when needed.

To be Starr.

The apartment was quiet except for the hum of the city outside. Lilly sat cross-legged on the couch, makeup wiped clean, hair twisted into a lazy knot. Charlotte curled up on the floor beneath the window, her wineglass cupped in both hands.

"I can't sleep," Charlotte said finally.

"You will. Eventually. Then you'll sleep too much. Then not at all. It's a cycle."

Charlotte turned toward her. "Do you remember your first week?"

Lilly gave a low chuckle. "Yeah. I wore silver heels three sizes too big and almost broke my ankle walking to the pole. My first client tipped me with Canadian money."

Charlotte smiled softly. "Did you cry?"

"Only in the bathroom. Only into my drink. Only when no one was watching." She paused. "Same as you."

They sat in silence for a while, the kind that stretches and softens between women who've seen too much too young.

Charlotte looked at her, voice low. "Do you think I'm changing?"

Lilly studied her for a beat too long. "Yes."

Charlotte's throat tightened. "Is that bad?"

"No," Lilly said. "But it's dangerous."

Charlotte nodded slowly, as if she already knew that. Her fingers traced the rim of her glass. "I don't know who I am right now."

"You're between versions of yourself," Lilly said, her voice gentler now. "That's what this job does. It strips you down. Forces you to choose what pieces you want to keep and what you're willing to sell."

Charlotte met her eyes. "What if I lose the wrong pieces?"

"Then we pick them up when you're ready," Lilly said. "If you make it that far."

Charlotte didn't speak after that. She just stared out the window again, watching New York breathe its lights flickering like cigarette embers, its heart beating fast like hers.

She didn't know who she was becoming.
But she knew the girl from home was already too far behind to follow.

Chapter 3: The Girl in the Mirror

The mirror didn't lie.

It was brutal, unflinching. The kind of truth that didn't ask permission.

Charlotte stared at herself like she was a stranger. The reflection was a girl with hollowed cheeks, eyeliner smudged like bruises, and lips cracked from cheap lipstick and forced smiles. She looked older than she had a week ago, like the club had already carved something out of her.

She reached up, touched her own face, fingertips brushing over the image like she could peel herself off the glass and step back into the girl she used to be. The one who smiled with her whole body. The one who danced for joy, not money.

But that girl was gone. Or hiding.

Now there was Starr.

And Starr had eyes that didn't blink when men stared too long. She had hands that knew how to slide money from pockets with grace. She had a mouth that whispered promises it never intended to keep.

She'd become her own invention. And it scared her how easy it was.

"Staring too long at yourself in here'll drive you crazy," Aliana said from her vanity, stroking mascara onto her lashes like war paint.

Charlotte didn't look away. "I think I'm already halfway there."

Aliana gave a soft grunt. "Then maybe you'll make it in this place after all."

The club pulsed like a beating heart - dark, alive, and full of secrets.

Tonight, the air was heavier. The perfume and sweat, the velvet and smoke, all stitched together in a scent that clung to skin like memory. The walls breathed in rhythm with the music. Bodies moved together but never truly touched. Everyone was looking, reaching, needing.

Charlotte stepped onto the floor and it swallowed her whole.

Men sat like gods on their leather thrones, drinks sweating in their hands, money folded and tucked like offerings. Their eyes searched for something to make them feel powerful again. Young again. Wanted again.

She felt them looking at her hungry, silent, devouring.

She walked like she owned the room, though inside, her chest was tight and her mouth was dry. Every step was a lie. Every smile was a bruise waiting to form.

But the money? The money was real.

Meanwhile the floor was pulsing with its own stories to tell.

Jennifer was straddling a regular with slow, deliberate movements her lips near his ear, her hands sliding along his neck like silk. She gave a wink as Charlotte passed, mouthing, fake it till it feels good.

Inga was in the dressing room crying again her sobs muffled by a towel. No one asked why. They'd heard it all before. Back home. Sick kids. Broken promises. A husband that stopped calling. Everyone in that place had a wound they kept hidden under fishnets and glitter.

Charlotte wanted to scream.

Instead, she reapplied her lip gloss.

She found Dylan in the hallway again, leaned against the wall like he'd been carved into the building.

His shirt was half-unbuttoned, tie loose around his neck. He looked like a rich boy playing a poor man's game and winning.

"You look like hell," he said.

She raised an eyebrow. "You look like temptation."

He grinned. "Flattery won't get you out of a lap dance."

"I'm not selling anything tonight."

He stepped closer, his voice lower. "Everyone here is selling something. Don't lie to me."

His nearness was a challenge. His breath smelled like bourbon and defiance.

"You think I'm naïve?" she asked.

"I think you're dangerous," he said. "Because you still believe there's a way out."

She swallowed hard. "There isn't?"

He stared at her, the smile fading just a little. "Not for girls who wait too long to run.
She didn't reply. But something cold settled in her spine.

Later a man in a gray suit asked her to dance like it was a favor he was granting her. His hands stayed in his lap. His wedding ring gleamed under the red lights like an accusation.
He didn't speak. Just watched her move like she was a shadow on a screen. A shape, not a person. When the song ended, he pressed a hundred-dollar bill into her hand and whispered, "You remind me of my daughter."
She didn't know whether to vomit or cry.
She shoved the bill into her bra and walked out without looking back.

At Lilly's place, she peeled off her lashes like scabs, sat on the cold bathroom floor, and stared at herself in the mirror again. Her face was bare now. No glitter. No mask. Just skin. Just bone. Just a tired girl with aching feet and too many secrets.
Lilly came in, tossed her a hoodie, and sat beside her. She opened a beer and handed it over.
Charlotte took it with shaking hands. "I feel like I'm turning into someone I don't recognize."

"That's the job."

"I thought it would be fun. Dangerous, maybe. But glamorous. I thought I'd feel powerful."

Lilly looked at her sideways. "And what do you feel?"

Charlotte's voice cracked. "Like a ghost in my own body."

Lilly didn't say anything for a while. Then she leaned her head back against the tub. "There's a line we all cross in here. The one between pretending and becoming."

Charlotte blinked hard. "And if I don't want to cross it?"

"Then you have to leave before it's too late."

The silence that followed felt like a warning.

Charlotte finished her beer and stared at the wall, tears burning but never falling.

She wasn't sure if she wanted to go back to being Charlotte. But she wasn't sure she could survive as Starr.

Chapter 4: Club Politics

The first time Charlotte held a thousand dollars in her hand, it didn't feel like money.
It felt like a secret. A confession someone had whispered into her palm and told her to keep safe. It smelled like ambition masked by cologne, like fear buried under lust. It was still warm from the hands it had passed through greedy, lonely hands that clung to her body for seconds too long, looking for something they couldn't quite name.
It was her third night on the floor.
She had danced on stage, trembling, unsure of her own body. The lights were too bright. They painted her in shades of desire that didn't feel like her own. The pole was cold. Her grip was weak. The men didn't look at her - they consumed her.
But it wasn't the stage that paid. It was the hustle. She'd learned that fast.
Lilly had leaned close to her in the dressing room that night, cigarette dangling from her fingers even though smoking wasn't allowed.
"You waiting for a miracle or what?" she said with a crooked smile. "There is no money falling from heaven, sweetheart. You want to eat? Go hunt."
Charlotte blinked at her reflection. She barely recognized the girl in the mirror: lashes too long, lips too red, eyes already learning to fake it.

"What do I even say?" she asked.

"Doesn't matter," Lilly said. "Smile. Look hungry, but not desperate. Be soft. Let them think you like them. Ask about their wives, their kids, their business deals. Men love talking about their lives, especially when they're lying about them."
Charlotte took a breath. Nodded.
And walked out into the jungle.
She shadowed Lilly at first. Watched the way she floated from man to man, all liquid charm and effortless seduction. She never begged. She never lingered too long. If a guy wasn't biting, she'd slide away mid-sentence like smoke.
"You're not selling sex," Lilly whispered later that night, sipping her vodka cranberry like it was water. "You're selling yes. The possibility. The maybe. That's what they're paying for."
Charlotte tried to mimic the rhythm. She smiled. She laughed. She sat with men who stared at her chest and talked about their investments. She let her hand brush their knees. She let her lips part just enough to suggest secrets she'd never tell. She didn't lie, not exactly. She just told them the truth they wanted to hear.

That night, she made $1,240.
More than she had made in the last two months back home scrubbing counters, pouring coffee, folding discount jeans at the mall.

When they left the club at 4 a.m., the city was dead quiet. A chill still hung in the early spring air. Charlotte's stockings were torn, and her heels dangled from her hand. Her purse was heavy.

"I feel like I robbed someone," she said.

Lilly laughed. "You didn't rob anyone, baby. They paid to pretend you cared. And you gave them a show."

Charlotte looked down at her hands, the cash still tingling between her fingers. Something had shifted. Something had cracked open. The money wasn't just money - it was permission. It was proof that she could do this. That she could become whoever she needed to be to survive.

By the end of her first week, Charlotte was fluent in the game.

She'd learned the language the smiles, the glances, the subtle lean of the hip. She'd figured out who tipped well, who only watched, who'd waste your time. She stopped feeling guilty for pretending to care.

She stopped pretending to feel guilty.

There was a rhythm to the club. A strange, glitter-drenched ballet.

Melody flirted like she was sixteen bright eyes, biting her lip, lots of giggles. Inga, with her ice-queen persona and piercing blue eyes, barely spoke a word to customers unless she wanted something. Jennifer had mom energy soft hands, fake concern, a comforting touch on the knee while she drained their wallets with practiced grace. Amy was a beast: cutthroat, drop-dead gorgeous, and utterly ruthless.

Charlotte found her own style in the spaces between them. She didn't try to be anyone she wasn't. She let them see the small-town girl who still flinched at hard stares. The one who looked like maybe, just maybe, he could still be saved. It worked.

"Your vulnerability is your weapon," Lilly said one night in the dressing room. "Use it. Bleed just enough to get their attention. Then close the wound before they see too much."

The money started to stack. Slowly at first, then faster.

Charlotte learned how to walk the floor, how to read a man, how to tell when someone was trying to play her. She learned the weight of a good night and the sting of a slow one. She learned the hunger in her belly wasn't always about food.

The club had its own rules. Its own universe.

You couldn't see it at first. When you were new, everything looked the same: neon and noise, sweat and sparkle, heels clicking on marble floors, the smell of vanilla lotion mixed with body heat. But beneath the surface was a whole other structure. A quiet, invisible caste system built on looks, loyalty, hustle, and luck.

At the top were the VIP girls.

Untouchable. Unbothered. They didn't run to customers, they let customers crawl to them. They didn't hustle on the floor or swing around the pole for attention. They barely danced anymore. Their stage sets were symbolic, five-minute rituals that reminded the rest of the club who really ran the room. A spin here. A hair flip there. Then a slow walk back into the shadows, where the real money waited.

They were always dressed like they were about to board a private jet. Skirts tight, nails sharp, perfume heavy and expensive. You could smell Baccarat or Tom Ford on them before they turned a corner. Their lashes were curled to the sky, their faces glazed in glassy highlight. They never looked tired, even when you knew they hadn't slept.
Some of them, like Melody, had been at the club so long that stories swirled around her like urban legend.
Melody had three "boyfriends," each one thinking he was the only one. One paid for her penthouse. One leased her a G-Wagon. The third wired her monthly "allowance" just to talk. She barely lifted a finger anymore. She had a table reserved every Friday and Saturday, and no one else was allowed

to sit there not even the managers questioned it. That was Melody's kingdom.

"I don't sell dances," she once said flatly, applying lipstick in the mirror. "I sell illusion. And they're happy to pay for it."
It was hard not to watch her. Not to want her life. Charlotte found herself staring sometimes, studying how Melody moved slow, deliberate, unbothered. Her laugh was low and slow, like she already knew the punchline to every joke.

Aliana called her a masterclass in manipulation. "She knows exactly how to let a man think he's winning while she's gutting him."
Melody's world felt like a dream. But there was something ghostly about it too.
She didn't talk to the new girls. She didn't sit in the dressing room unless she had to. She arrived late, left earlier than most. There was a coldness to her, a distance, like someone who had floated too far above the clouds to remember what gravity felt like.
"She was sweet once," Lilly said one night, watching Melody from across the dressing room. "Before she learned how to disappear."

And then there was Anna.
Where Melody was cold and calculated, Inga was fire. Russian, blonde, body like a statue carved out

of lust. Her accent was thick and deliberate. She knew how to turn it up when men leaned in closer. She had a diamond tennis bracelet she claimed was from an oil tycoon she met at the Four Seasons.

"You just have to make them feel important," Inga told Charlotte during a smoke break. "They don't want you to be real. They want a fantasy. So, give them the fantasy. But don't ever get caught believing in it yourself."

Anna had one customer who'd been coming to see her every Saturday for three years. He'd bought her a Rolex. Paid off her credit cards. Flew her to Miami for a weekend just to watch her tan.
He called her "my little goddess."
She called him "number six."

These girls weren't just dancers they were myths inside the club.
Stories about them passed through the dressing room like scripture. One girl claimed she saw Amy leave with a Saudi prince in a Rolls-Royce. Another swore Melody had a real estate agent who brought cash to the club just to sit next to her. Someone even said Valery was being flown out to Dubai once a month and had a "no dancing" clause in her contract.

Whether it was true or not didn't matter. The legend was enough to make every girl ache with envy and hope.

Charlotte used to watch them, wondering what separated them from her. Was it just looks? Was it timing? Was it sheer, unapologetic shamelessness? Lilly told her the truth one night, when they were taking off their lashes side by side after a long shift.

"They learned the game early. That you don't chase money. You make it chase you. You keep the mystery alive. You never give too much. And you never break character."

Charlotte nodded, her reflection tired, glitter clinging to the hollows beneath her eyes.

"And if you do?" she asked softly.

Lilly paused. "You become one of us."

This elite tier of dancers existed in a different time zone. They weren't concerned with competition. They didn't fight for stage time or dance cards. They had managers texting them directly when clients arrived. They were always "requested."

They didn't dance for twenty-dollar tips. They didn't flirt for free. They didn't waste words.

And they definitely didn't fall in love.

Because love was expensive. And they'd already sold too many pieces of themselves to afford that kind of loss again.

Then there were the workhorses.
The spine of the club. The quiet machines behind the noise and chaos. The girls who didn't need to scream to be seen. They weren't flashy like the VIP queens, and they didn't chase the drama or the spotlight. But they were always there. Reliable. Ruthless in their discipline. Clocking in. Cashing out. Making money like a religion.

Lilly was one of them. Aliana too.

And Charlotte was starting to understand that while the VIP girls ruled from their thrones, the workhorses built the fucking palace.
They came in with their gym bags slung over one shoulder, headphones in, no makeup yet, hair tied up. Their faces were bare until it was time to transform. There was a calm around them, a kind of seasoned stillness that said I've done this a thousand times, and I'll do it a thousand more. Lilly had that look when she walked through the dressing room door. Not a strut, not a slouch, just a slow, grounded, unbothered presence. She changed at her own pace. Bra off, lashes on, then she'd lean in close to the mirror and line her lips with surgical precision.

She never rushed.

Because she didn't have to.

Charlotte had started to notice how the other girls moved around Lilly. Not scared, exactly, but careful. Like they knew she was watching even when she wasn't looking. Lilly didn't gossip. She didn't fight. But if you crossed her, she wouldn't raise her voice she'd just stop speaking to you, and your name would evaporate from the room like cigarette smoke. She had a long memory and a short list of people she trusted.

Charlotte had once seen a new girl make the mistake of stealing a regular from Lilly tried to slide into his lap like she owned the place. Lilly didn't say a word. She just watched, smiled, and let the girl finish her set. The next week, that same girl couldn't get a drink, a customer, or a second of peace. The whispers started. The DJ never called her name right. Her locker was mysteriously locked one night when she needed it most.

That's how power worked when you were a workhorse. Quiet. Relentless. Efficient.

Aliana was another one. Built like an athlete, moved like a soldier. She could flip herself upside down on the pole, hang by one ankle, and still make eye contact with a guy drinking tequila in the corner. She didn't bother with flirtation unless it served a purpose. She was here to work.

And she had rules.

No sleeping with customers. No borrowing money. No bringing your problems onto the floor. She treated the club like a battleground, and her body was both her weapon and her armor. The only softness she showed was with Charlotte and even that was rare. But when Aliana talked to her, when she leaned in and gave advice, it landed like gospel.

"I don't get high at work," she told Charlotte one night, after watching another girl stumble out of the dressing room. "Because I don't need to numb it. I see this place. And when you see it clear, you don't stay longer than you need to."

That stuck with Charlotte. It cut through her haze, her hunger, her growing addiction to the rush. Because Aliana had been there long enough to know the difference between surviving the club and being swallowed by it.

The workhorses weren't glamorous.

They didn't get flown out or showered in Chanel bags.

But they ate.

They made more money than almost anyone because they treated it like a job, not a fantasy. They worked the floor like clockwork - knew which tables to hit and which to avoid. Knew how to spot a wallet from a mile away. Knew the signs of a man about to fall in love and how to stop it before it became a problem.

They knew when to talk. When to listen. When to laugh. When to leave.

And they always tipped. The DJ. The house mom. Security. Bartenders. Bouncers. They kept the wheels greased, their names good, and their exits clean.

No mess. No drama. No stories floating back to management.

They were respected.

Because everyone knew they could outlast you. Out-earn you. Outsmart you. And if they wanted, they could end you with a glance, a whisper, a single moment of indifference.

To Charlotte, the workhorses were what real strength looked like.

They weren't goddesses like the VIP girls. They didn't float above the fray. They were the fray. They knew the weight of every dollar and the cost of every compromise.

They knew how to fake intimacy and walk away without guilt. How to smile through exhaustion. How to stay sober in a room full of poison.

They were survivors. Not just of the club, but of life. You could see it in their eyes. The way they scanned a room like they'd been betrayed before. The way they laughed, full-bodied but guarded.

The way they carried themselves like they'd
already died once and come back harder.
Charlotte didn't know yet which path she
belonged to. But she found herself drawn to their
fire. Their discipline. Their unwavering sense of
purpose.
Because deep down, Charlotte didn't want to be
worshipped.
She wanted to be feared.
She wanted to know how to walk through hell in
heels and come out clean.
And the workhorses? They were already doing it.

Below them were the floaters.
The new girls. The part-timers. The burnout cases.
The broken-winged birds who fluttered in, dazzled
by the lights, only to find themselves swallowed
by the shadows. They weren't rooted in the game
like the workhorses, and they didn't play it like the
VIPs. They were in-between, caught in the
undertow of survival and illusion.
You could spot them instantly.
The way they hesitated in heels. The way they
clutched their bags like a lifeline. The way their
eyes scanned the room too quickly, too often -
searching for something that would never appear.

They were the ones who always ended up crying
in the dressing room by midnight.

Some of them came in bright-eyed, hopeful, thinking the money would be easy, the glamour real, the danger overstated. Others arrived already frayed at the edges: numb, hollow, halfway-gone before they even put on the heels.

Lola was one of the newest. Nineteen. Pretty in a fragile, almost translucent way. Big brown eyes, soft cheeks, the kind of innocence that made men generous, but also dangerous.

She wore too much perfume. Her makeup always smudged under the lights. She kept a tiny notebook in her locker with "GOALS" scribbled in bubble letters: Pay off credit card. Help mom. Buy car.

She said she was only dancing for the summer. But summer had come and gone, and she was still there. Still asking how to upsell a champagne room. Still borrowing lashes and body glitter. Still crying in the mirror when a customer ghosted her after promising the world.

Lilly tried to guide her at first, but it was like throwing a life vest into a hurricane. Lola wanted to believe the lies, wanted to believe she was different. That she could bend the rules, charm her way into success without the armor the other girls had built.

She once told Charlotte, in a rare, broken moment, "I just want someone to pick me. You know? Really pick me. Not just rent me."

It was the kind of line that stayed with you. Haunted you. Because it was honest. And because most of them had felt it, too.

Samantha was different.
Older. Maybe thirty. Maybe more. She never said. She came in late, left early, didn't talk much. Her sets were half-hearted, her hustle lukewarm. You could tell she'd once been sharp, fierce maybe even one of the VIP girls in another life, but something had dulled her.
Her stilettos were scuffed. Her extensions tangled. Her laugh hollow.
She worked three nights a week and spent most of her time in the corner of the dressing room, scrolling through her phone like she was looking for something lost.
Some nights she made good money enough to remind the others she still had it in her. But more often than not, she left frustrated. Bitter. Muted.
"I'm just tired," she told Charlotte one night, zipping up her thigh-high boots with a wince. "Not just in my body. In my soul. This place… it takes something from you. Every fucking shift. And I think I'm finally out of things to give."

She wasn't dramatic about it. Just honest. And that was scarier than any meltdown.

And then there was Gia.

Half fire, half mess. Beautiful in that chaotic, devastating way like a cigarette still burning on silk sheets. She had tattoos winding up her spine, long red hair, and a habit of drinking tequila straight from the bottle while reapplying her lip liner in the mirror.

She flirted with everyone. Fought with most. She once slapped a customer across the face for calling her the wrong name and danced two songs later like nothing happened.

Gia had the kind of magnetism that came with deep damage. You could feel it vibrating off her skin this dangerous pull toward pleasure and destruction.

"I'm here because I don't know where else I belong," she confessed to Charlotte once, sitting on the floor of the dressing room, her fishnets ripped at the thigh, mascara bleeding down one cheek. "And I keep thinking if I can just make enough money, I'll figure it out. But I never do. I just buy prettier cages."

She smiled when she said it. A smile with no joy in it.

Just teeth.

The floaters lived shift to shift.

They took what they could, gave more than they should, and held onto the hope that the next night would be better. That someone would notice them. Save them. Love them. Pay them.

But the club didn't save anyone.

It watched. It waited. It fed on vulnerability and poured glitter over the wounds.

Some floaters found their footing hardened, evolved, climbed up. Others slipped quietly out of rotation. Their names forgotten. Their lockers emptied like they'd never existed at all.

Charlotte saw them like ghosts.

Like the version of herself she feared she might still become.

And so, every night, she danced just a little harder. Hustled just a little sharper. Because she knew the club didn't offer mercy.

It only gave you choices.

Evolve. Or disappear.

The house mom's name was Darla. She was in her late forties, wore pink Crocs, and had seen every version of every girl a place like this could chew up and spit out. She kept a drawer full of safety pins, mints, lashes, tampons, and Advil. She patched broken costumes and broken hearts with the same tired hands.

Charlotte quickly learned that Darla was the closest thing to a mother figure the club had and tipping her wasn't optional. Neither was tipping the DJ or the security guys. The unspoken rule: you want to be safe, played on time, and seen in a good light? Show respect. In cash.

"Ten to the DJ, fifteen to Darla, twenty if she fixed your top," Lilly said. "And security? They throw a guy out for you, you better hand them something."

Charlotte nodded. Her mind felt like a ledger now: dollars in, dollars out, all of it part of the cost of staying alive in this world. You paid to be protected. You paid to be seen. You paid to be allowed to exist here.

The DJ's name was Brick, which wasn't a nickname - just a bad decision by someone's mother. He had a lazy voice and a thing for Amy, who used it to her full advantage.

"Play something with a drop," Charlotte told him once, before her second stage set.

He raised a brow. "You tip first?"

She slid him a twenty. The bass hit harder than ever that night.

It was just after 2 AM on a Thursday. The club had thinned out, the music had slowed, and the energy had shifted from high-octane glamour to something rawer. More real.

Charlotte was in the dressing room, sitting on the cracked leather couch with her heels off and her legs curled beneath her, counting singles and rubbing the soreness from her arches. The air was heavy with hairspray, perfume, and exhaustion. That's when she saw Lola in the mirror. The girl was hunched at her station, trying to reapply lip gloss with shaking hands. Her eyes were glassy. Her cheeks were blotchy. The kind of quiet collapse that didn't make noise, but filled the room like smoke.

Charlotte watched her for a second, then stood and crossed the room.

"You okay?" she asked softly, crouching beside her.

Lola flinched like she'd forgotten other people existed. She sniffled, smiled too fast, and wiped at her face with the back of her hand.

"Yeah, yeah. Just tired. Just... ugh, I'm being dumb. It's nothing."

Charlotte didn't answer. Just waited.

Lola looked down at her lap. Her hands were clenched tight around her phone. On the screen was a message thread one-sided. Dozens of blue bubbles, all unanswered. The last one read: Are you still coming tonight? I saved the room for you.

Charlotte felt her chest tighten. She sat beside Lola, shoulder to shoulder, and didn't say anything for a moment. Just breathed with her.

"I used to cry in this room every night," she said finally. "I'd go on stage and smile like I owned the world, then come back here and unravel. I thought it would get better. That if I was prettier, or better at talking, or wore something tighter, they'd stay. They never stayed."

Lola turned toward her, mascara smudged, eyes watery. "Why do they lie like that?" she whispered. "He said he'd bring me to Miami. He said he wanted to take care of me. I believed him."

Charlotte reached out and took the girl's hand, gently unclenching her fingers.

"Because they can. Because we let them. And sometimes… sometimes we want the lie more than we want the truth."

Silence.

Lola's lip trembled. "I don't know if I can do this."

Charlotte looked her dead in the eyes.

"You can. But you have to learn the rules. You have to stop giving them the part of you that cries in this room. You sell the fantasy. You keep your heart in your locker."

Lola nodded slowly, swallowing hard.

"Will you help me?" she asked, voice cracking like a child's.

Charlotte hesitated. She wanted to say yes. She wanted to take this girl and pull her out of the fire. But she also knew this place didn't save people. It devoured them. And nobody could swim for two.

"I'll walk with you," Charlotte said, squeezing her hand. "But you have to learn to run on your own."

They sat there a moment longer. Two girls,
covered in glitter and heartbreak, holding on like
maybe that was enough.
And then the DJ called Charlotte's name.
The music thumped back to life. Another round.
Another dance. Another lie to sell.

Charlotte stood up and looked back one last time.
Lola was reapplying her lip gloss. Not perfectly.
But steadier.
It wasn't a rescue.
But maybe it was a beginning.

Chapter 5: Money talks

By mid-April, the money started feeling normal.
So did the ache in her calves and the smell of
sweat and perfume mixed with stale champagne.
The nights bled into each other. The stories from
men started to overlap. Divorce. Heartbreak.
Loneliness. Success laced with emptiness.

Some nights, she felt like a therapist in lingerie.
Other nights, she felt like a ghost.
But the cash was real.
So, she stayed.
Charlotte was starting to learn the difference
between working and winning.
Working was what the new girls did aimless floor-
walking, awkward laughs, too much eye contact,
not enough confidence. Winning was when the
men came to you. When they knew your name
before you sat down. When the DJ called your
stage set and it felt like thunder.
Amy was a winner.
She knew how to corner a man without even
standing up. One look, one slow swirl of her straw,
and they'd rise like hypnotized dogs. Rumor was
she'd pulled a married hedge fund guy into VIP
three times in one night and left with ten grand.

"She's dangerous," Aliana told Charlotte once, adjusting her corset in the mirror. "Pretty girls who know they're pretty always are."

Charlotte nodded, watching Amy walk by with that lethal sway in her hips. She was a panther in platforms smooth, sharp, untouchable.
Aliana, on the other hand, was different. Soft where others were sharp. Protective. Loyal. She made sure Charlotte never walked alone to the train. She checked her tips after every shift, helped her fix her lashes in the bathroom, kept her close when the crowd got loud.
"You don't owe these men shit," Aliana whispered in her ear once when a customer grabbed her wrist too hard. "They want something? Make them pay."
There was power in that. In the way Aliana stood her ground. In the way she made you feel like maybe you weren't just meat in glitter.
Still, the tension among the dancers was thick enough to slice.
Girls competed for the same men, the same rooms, the same dollars.
Smiles could turn into snarls fast.
Charlotte saw it happen on a Friday.
Valery and Jennifer were working the same table - a group of Wall Street boys already swimming in vodka and testosterone. Charlotte walked by just in time to hear it.

"You stole my client," Jennifer hissed.

Valery smirked. "He invited me."

"Bullshit."

Their voices rose until a floor manager stepped in, whispering something sharp and final in Valery's ear. She walked away furious, heels clacking too hard against the floor.

Charlotte turned back toward the bar, her stomach tight.

This place could be paradise and purgatory all at once.

There was a hierarchy.

Not just between the dancers, but in every crack of the building.

The floor managers had their favorites. Some girls got better stage times. Better booths. Better protection.

The top earners got more freedom. Fewer rules. A longer leash.

"Don't rock the boat," Lilly told her. "This place loves money. If you make it, they'll leave you alone. If you don't, they'll find someone who does."

Charlotte started hustling harder.

She didn't wait for eye contact anymore. She took it. She leaned into conversations. She learned how to plant her hand just right on a shoulder or thigh. How to ask about their day like she gave a damn.

Sometimes she did give a damn. And that scared her.

The line between the act and the actress was fading.

The club was like a microcosm of a strange, glittering universe where everything had its price. And the currency wasn't just money - it was power, status, attention. A hierarchy of survival that wasn't as clear as it seemed.

Lilly was the queen of this kingdom. Not because she was the best dancer. Not because she had the most cash. But because she was untouchable. She could sit with the richest men in the room and make them feel like the most important person in the world, and then walk away with a tip that made Charlotte's weekly paycheck look like pocket change.

But Lilly had something else, something Charlotte hadn't realized until she watched her in action for the first time.

Lilly had control over every situation. Every interaction. She had this uncanny ability to read people: their weaknesses, their desires, their fears - and exploit them. It wasn't just about seduction. It was about domination. A game of psychological warfare that no one else seemed to know they were even playing.

And Charlotte was starting to see how dangerous that game could be.

Charlotte's first regular was a man named Neil.
He wore his wedding band like a shield flashing
silver under the dim lights, the kind of ring that
said "I made promises I'm still trying to keep." On
the opposite wrist, a Rolex caught the pulse of the
room, its face gleaming every time he raised a
glass of neat scotch to his lips. He wasn't young.
Late forties, maybe. Salt-and-pepper hair cropped
short, skin smooth but tired around the eyes. He
was put together, always in a pressed button-
down, always smelling like cedar and something
expensive and cold.

He sat alone in the same corner every Friday. Near
the VIP entrance. Not too close to the chaos, but
never far from it either. Like someone watching a
fire, half hoping it would jump the grate.
Charlotte noticed him before he noticed her.
There was something about the way he held
himself: shoulders relaxed, but not soft. He didn't
scan the room like the other men. Didn't ogle or
beckon or lick his lips. He just watched,
unreadable, sipping his drink like it was all one
long, slow movie he couldn't look away from.
The night they met, she almost didn't go up to
him. She was still learning to read the floor, still
getting the scent of money and loneliness on her
tongue. But something about Neil felt... familiar.
Not safe. But stable. Like a winter coat left out for
you on the porch.

He looked up when she approached, eyes the color of smoke and river stones.

"You're new," he said. Not a question. A fact.

"Yeah," she replied, easing into the seat beside him. "That obvious?"

He gave her a tired smile. "You haven't learned to pretend you're not cold yet."

That caught her off guard. She laughed. A real one.

The conversation unraveled from there. Slowly. Gently. He asked where she was from, and when she told him, he nodded like he cared, even though he had no idea where the town was. She mentioned her mom's perfume. Her dad's silence. The way the bus smelled like warm plastic and regret.

He never touched her. Not once.

Just listened.

And when she stood to leave, he slipped five hundred into her hand and said, "See you next Friday."

That became their rhythm.

Fridays.

She started to look forward to them, not just for the money, though that was nice. But for the calm. The way he never asked for more than what she gave. The way she didn't have to fake a laugh or a moan or pretend she liked being groped by some stranger in a booth.

With Neil, she could breathe.

What Charlotte didn't know, at least not at first, was what he left behind to sit in that velvet corner with her each week.

A wife. Two daughters. A mortgage in Westchester. A golden retriever named Max who waited at the front door every night for him to come home.

He was a partner at a law firm. The kind with wood-paneled offices and a view of the East River. He had lunch meetings and country club dues and people who shook his hand too hard and told him he was "a damn good man."

But at night, once a week, he slipped off his life like a heavy coat and came to the club, where no one expected him to fix anything.

Charlotte never asked what he did outside. And he never offered.

But over time, bits of him cracked through.

Once, he mentioned he used to play piano. His mother forced lessons on him until his hands were too big for delicate things. Another time, he told her his youngest daughter liked painting horses, even though she'd never seen one in real life.

"I think she wants to be somewhere else," he said quietly, staring into his glass. "She's just too young to know it's okay."

Charlotte understood that.

Because so was she.

He never asked for VIP. Never took her out. Never crossed the line.
But there were moments, small, burning ones - where the air between them shifted.
One night, she caught him watching her dance. Just watching. Not like a customer, but like a man remembering what it felt like to want something he couldn't name.
Afterward, she sat beside him, still glitter-drenched and out of breath. He reached for her hand, just lightly, like someone testing if a flame still burned.
"You look sad tonight," he said.
She didn't respond.
Because she was.
And because with Neil, she didn't have to lie about it.
Charlotte didn't know what that said about him. Or about her.
But something about those Friday nights felt dangerously comforting. He didn't try to own her. He didn't pretend she was something she wasn't. He just let her be. And in a place where everything was sold, bartered, or stripped away, that felt like the most expensive gift of all.
She began to crave it.
Not him. Not exactly.

But the feeling. The illusion of intimacy without the risk. The attention without the cost. It was addictive in its own way.

He made her feel seen.

And seen was dangerous.

Because being seen meant being known. And being known meant someone might notice the cracks beneath the glitter, the hunger behind the eyes, the girl beneath the name.

Chapter 6: Lines on Glass

The night Valery pulled Charlotte into the bathroom was the beginning of something that didn't have a name yet, just a feeling.
It was almost 3 AM, and the floor was chaos. Stilettos clacked across the sticky marble. Bass pounded like a second heartbeat. A group of drunk hedge fund guys were throwing money like it was burning their fingers, and Charlotte had just come off a dance with one of them, her skin still hot, her knees sore.
Valery slipped her a look from across the dressing room mirror. Cool. Controlled. Dangerous in that detached way only the VIP girls could be. Her hair always on point, makeup done to the perfection. A Louis Vuitton bag sat at her feet. She didn't smile often.
"Come with me," she said simply, nodding toward the back.
Charlotte followed.

The bathroom was too clean for what happened in it. White tiles. Gold accents. A long granite counter lined with expensive lotions and perfumes stolen or gifted or bartered. Valery locked the door behind them and turned up the music on her phone to drown out whatever might be heard.

She reached into her purse, pulled out a compact mirror, and laid it flat on the sink.

Charlotte watched in silence as Valery shook out a tiny zip lock bag. The white powder dusted the mirror like powdered sugar. Then came the card: swift, practiced. Two perfect lines. Clean. Sharp.

Valery looked up at her.

"You dance better on this."

Charlotte blinked. Her throat dried up.

"I've never"

"You will."

And just like that, she passed her a hundred-dollar bill, rolled tight.

Charlotte hesitated. Not out of fear. But because something inside her whispered this is a door.

Once you walk through, you don't come back the same.

But she was tired. Her legs ached. Her chest felt too full with things she didn't have the words for.

She bent down. Inhaled.

And the world snapped into crystal.

The high was subtle at first. Then full-body. Like her blood had been replaced with electricity. Her heartbeat raced. Her lips tingled. Everything felt sharper, sharper than it had in weeks. The music, the lights, the way her dress hugged her body, it was all more.

Back on the floor, she floated.

She laughed louder, touched softer, danced harder. Customers couldn't get enough. She made almost a thousand dollars in the next two hours alone. It felt like cheating. Like magic.
She was hooked before she even knew she wanted more.

The following nights blurred.
She and Valery would slip off between sets, or in the corners of the dressing room when no one was looking. Sometimes it was Samantha or Gia who tagged along. Coke made them fast. Made them focused. Made them invincible.
The mornings were hell: dry mouth, cracked lips, mascara smudged under sunglasses. But they faded quickly under the next rush.
Charlotte started working longer hours. Skipping meals. She grew thinner. Her cheekbones sharpened. Her eyes sparkled too much.
The money was insane. She could feel it in the weight of her bag when she got home. The buzz of the bills in her hand. She sent some to her mom. Tucked some away in an envelope under her mattress. Bought a new pair of red-bottoms just to feel like she belonged.
But her laugh started to change. A little too loud. A little too late.
So did her eyes.

Rob noticed.

It was a Tuesday when he called her into the office.

She was still wired from the weekend, her leg bouncing in place. The room smelled like aftershave and the faint hint of old paperwork. Rob sat behind the desk, his hands folded, eyes soft but serious.

"You okay, Starr?" he asked.

She smiled too fast. "Yeah. Killing it out there. Why?"

He looked at her for a long second.

"You're burning too hot."

She blinked. "What does that mean?"

He didn't answer immediately. Just leaned forward a little, his voice lower now.

"I've seen girls go up like fireworks in this place. Bright. Beautiful. Fast. And then they're gone. One bad night. One bad habit. One guy who takes too much."

Charlotte said nothing.

"I'm not your dad," Rob said gently. "But I've been here long enough to know when someone's trying to outrun something. This place'll feed that. Until it doesn't."

She nodded. Smiled again. "I'm fine."

He sighed. "Just... keep your head, okay?"

She left before he could say anything else.

That night, she did three lines before midnight. The music thumped louder. The money came faster.

She told herself she was still in control.

And that was the first lie she started to believe.

That Friday night, Charlotte showed up already high.

She'd barely slept the night before, three hours maybe, but sleep felt like something for people with regular lives. She walked into the club like she owned it, strutting through the side entrance in six-inch heels, hair curled to perfection, eyes rimmed with smoky kohl. Her lips glistened. Her skin shimmered.

Anna handed her a mini Dior perfume bottle filled with vodka and winked. "For later."

The music was already pulsing when Charlotte stepped onto the floor. Lights flashed in violet and gold. The crowd was thick - finance bros on a bender, women in birthday sashes screaming over champagne, older men watching everything with quiet hunger.

Charlotte felt electric.

Everything moved in slow motion, then hyper speed. Her heart beat like a war drum. Her movements were silk and fire. She danced like her body wasn't hers, like something had taken over - some wild, sensual force that lived only in the shadows.

Valery passed her in the hallway, tossed a $100 tip on her chest like a game. "He wants you again," she whispered, pointing toward a VIP booth.

Charlotte didn't ask who. She didn't need to.

Inside the VIP lounge, the lights were lower, the air thicker. Cigar smoke curled in ribbons. Bottles sparkled in ice buckets. A man in a tailored black suit was leaning back in the corner. Grey temples. Gold chain. Smile like he paid people to smile for him. A new one. She didn't even catch his name.

He ran a finger down her arm and said, "You look expensive."

She leaned in close. "That's because I am."

He liked that. They all did.

She slid into his lap, felt the weight of cash waiting in his pocket. He smelled like oud and success. She pretended to care about what he did for a living. He pretended not to stare at her chest. It was a game. And she was good at it.

By midnight, she'd made over $2,000.

Gia handed her a silver flask in the dressing room. "To nights we don't remember," she toasted.

Valery laid out another line on the counter. "To money we don't deserve."

Charlotte snorted it without blinking.

Back on the floor, her body hummed like it was plugged into the speakers. The pole welcomed her like an old lover. She flipped upside down, the crowd roaring beneath her. Every movement was precise, every grind, every twirl calculated to extract desire. She could feel them watching, not just the men, but the women, the dancers, the staff. She was no longer the new girl. She was Starr.

For a few hours, she forgot her small town. Forgot the duffle bag. Forgot the bus. Forgot the motel with the flickering light.

She was glitter and sweat and power.

At 4 AM, her feet were bleeding in her heels, but she didn't care.

She sat in the back dressing room, a wad of crumpled bills in her lap, mascara smudged under her lashes. Her body buzzing, teeth grinding slightly. Her reflection looked otherworldly: pale, glossy, radiant in the way only firework ashes are right before they vanish.

Samantha collapsed next to her, laughing. "Girl, you were on one tonight."

Charlotte smiled. "I know."

And in that moment, she didn't feel broken. She felt dangerous.

She felt like she could live in this world forever.

It wasn't until 6:12 AM that she finally unlocked the apartment door.

The hallway was silent, washed in the blue light of early morning. Her heels clicked once, then were kicked off halfway to the couch. She dropped her

bag, the cash spilling slightly onto the floor. It glittered in the pale light like some kind of offering - currency earned through hours of seduction, adrenaline, and invisible wounds. Charlotte stood there for a second, still wearing her lashes, her lips dry and cracked. Her hands trembled as she poured a glass of water, spilling a little on the counter. She didn't clean it up.
In the bathroom, her reflection stared back, too bright, too sharp. Eyes wide, pupils still blown. Cheekbones too pronounced. Glitter clinging to her clavicles like aftershocks.

She stripped slowly: dress, bra, thong - letting the fabric fall in a trail behind her like she was walking away from someone else's body.

She sat on the edge of the tub and finally let the silence hit.
It was loud.
Her phone buzzed somewhere in her bag. Maybe a client. Maybe Valery. Maybe no one. She didn't check
Charlotte stared at her own knees. The small bruise forming under her right one. The faint scrape on her thigh. Her body had become a ledger of nights like this - every mark a transaction.
She thought of Rob's voice.
"You're burning too hot."

For the first time, she wondered what it would feel like to burn out.
Not in flames. Not in drama.
Just… quietly.
To disappear under the surface of it all.
She turned the shower on. Stepped in. Let the water wash the glitter off her skin, watched it swirl down the drain like gold dust, like nothing.
And for a second, just a second, she missed herself.

Chapter 7: The VIP Room

She didn't know what it would feel like.

She'd imagined it a hundred different ways - more glamorous, maybe. Or dangerous. But never this quiet. Never this heavy.

The hallway to the VIP rooms was colder than the rest of the club, like the temperature dropped on purpose. The bass from the main floor was muffled here, reduced to a distant heartbeat behind velvet curtains. A row of identical doors lined the corridor, sleek and dark and expensive. They didn't have numbers, just subtle gold letters above each arch: E, F, G... and Room H, where Starr stood now, ticket clutched tight in her hand like a boarding pass to another world.

Her jaw clenched. Her teeth ground. The coke was already rushing through her, warm in the back of her throat, bitter on her gums. Valery had offered it between sets, like she was handing over a stick of gum. And Starr had taken it without thinking. Without hesitation. The tiny bag had disappeared between them like it was nothing.

It had started as something fun. Something to take the edge off.

But now it was armor.

And she needed armor tonight.

Her first VIP.

This was the place girls whispered about between sets. Where real money lived. Where boundaries blurred. Where masks either slipped or fused to the skin for good.

She swallowed the lump in her throat, straightened her back, and knocked.

The door swung open.

Inside, the room glowed gold low-lit sconces, a mirrored bar in the corner, deep red leather sofas that curved like lips. It was soundproofed, padded, insulated from the chaos outside. Time slowed in there. Nothing existed but this moment.

A man sat alone in the center of the couch, sipping something dark. Late forties, early fifties. Sharp suit. Black cufflinks. Expensive shoes. He didn't look up when she entered. Just held his glass mid-air and gestured.

"Close the door," he said.

She did.

He set the glass down carefully. Turned his head. And then he looked at her.

Not like the men on the floor who stared at her ass as she walked by. Not like the drunk guys who yelled compliments they didn't mean. He looked at her like he was about to open a gift he paid too much for.

"You're the new one," he said.

She nodded once. "Starr."

He chuckled. "Of course you are."

The silence stretched.

She moved closer.

It wasn't scripted, but it was choreography all the same: her hips rolling in slow rhythm to the ambient music that hummed through hidden speakers. Each step intentional. Her body language fluid, but calculated. A shift in the shoulders. A brush of fingertips against her own thigh. She could feel her pulse in her teeth.

She was supposed to seduce him. But right now, she was just trying not to pass out.

"Take your time," he said. "We've got an hour."

His voice was smooth. Confident. Not cruel. Not gentle. Just... neutral. Like he was ordering a meal.

She nodded and climbed onto his lap, knees sinking into the leather, her palms resting lightly on his chest. His cologne rose up like heat: bergamot and pepper and something smoky beneath it. He didn't touch her.

Not yet.

She felt her thighs tremble slightly

Her face was inches from his.

"First time?" he asked, not unkindly.

She didn't answer. Just met his eyes and started to move.

The performance was part muscle memory, part survival instinct. She traced her hands up her body slowly, inching her dress higher with each pass. She arched and dipped and teased. He watched. Quietly. No touching. Not yet.
And in that silence, her mind started screaming.

What the fuck am I doing here?

Her breath caught in her throat as she rolled her hips just above him. He exhaled audibly.
This isn't me. This is Starr. Charlotte doesn't do this.
But Charlotte did.
She was doing it now.
Her hands moved up his shoulders, then down again. She leaned in close, her lips grazing the shell of his ear.
He shivered.
So did she.
For a moment, she wasn't in the club. She was back in her childhood bedroom, sitting on a twin bed with the pink quilt. She could smell the dryer sheets her mom used. She could see the stuffed animal in the corner, the posters on the wall. She could hear her dad yelling downstairs: something about money.
And now here she was. Half-naked. Performing for a stranger.

A thousand miles away from everything she used to be.

And somehow, this felt safer than that house ever did.

He finally touched her - one hand, gentle, fingers trailing the curve of her waist. She let him. She didn't flinch. Not outwardly.

Inside, she shattered a little.

The trick was not to show it.

She slid off his lap and turned around, resting her back against his chest as she danced. His hands moved to her thighs. She kept breathing. Kept moving.

It wasn't erotic. It wasn't romantic. It was something else entirely transactional and sacred all at once. Power and vulnerability spinning in a tight circle.

When the hour ended, he stood, straightened his jacket, and handed her a stack of hundreds without making eye contact.

"Good girl," he said.

And then he was gone.

She sat alone in the room for five full minutes afterward, legs crossed, trying to catch her breath. Her makeup was intact. Her hair was fine. Nothing had happened that hadn't been allowed. But she felt scraped raw.

Not violated.

Not exactly.

Just… emptied.
Like she left part of herself in that leather couch and didn't know how to get it back.

That night, Dylan cornered her near the bar.
He wore his signature smirk polished white teeth; hair tousled just enough to look careless but perfect. A whisky in hand, sleeves rolled up, expensive watch flashing under the club lights.
"So," he said, leaning against the wall, "VIP now?"
She shrugged; voice cool. "You watching me?"
"Of course," he said, eyes raking over her. "I watch all the stars."
The flirtation dripped from his words, but his eyes weren't soft. There was something sharp in them - calculating.
She tilted her head. "I'm not your type."
"Don't be so sure." He took a sip. "But you're right. I like trouble. Melody's fun. Inga? Wild. But you…" He stepped closer. "You're different."
She didn't move. Didn't lean in or step away.
"I'm not here to be anyone's favorite mistake," she said quietly.
Dylan smiled like that only made her more interesting. "We'll see."

Later, Starr watched as he slid into a booth with Melody, his hand already on her thigh. Inga shot

her a knowing glance from across the room - lip
gloss perfect, laugh fake as hell.
Charlotte felt something twist in her chest.

Not jealousy.

Not yet.

But something colder. A warning, maybe.
That everyone wanted something. And nobody got
out clean.

Chapter 8: Fame in the Dark

Three months passed like a fever dream.

The nights blurred together, stitched by neon light and the relentless beat of trap music thudding through her veins. Time didn't pass like it used to. It folded in on itself, warped and melted by too much coke, too little sleep, too many lies told in too little fabric.

Starr had become a name.

Not just another girl in six-inch heels and body glitter, but the girl. The girl the high-rollers asked for. The girl the managers smiled at from across the floor. The girl with a rotation of regulars who lined up at the edge of the stage like worshippers at an altar.

Her photos were on the club's flyers now. Her name scrawled in glossy gold font. Rob gave her better spots. Even Steve nodded at her once when she walked past, an acknowledgment as heavy as a knighthood in their world.

And still, she felt empty.

Not lonely. Not sad. Just hollow. Like the higher she climbed, the less of herself she carried with her.

Money changed everything.

She'd never seen cash like this.

She learned how to tuck it into every crack of her life into her pillowcase, into her boot heel, into the back of her freezer. She spent it like she was afraid it might rot. Designer heels. Silk lingerie. Bottles of perfume that cost more than her old rent.
And blow.
So much blow.
It started with lines in the dressing room. Then in the bathroom stalls. Then casually on her makeup table at home while she redid her lipstick for the third time before work. It made her sharper, funnier, faster. It helped her stay up, stay sexy, stay Starr - the girl they all wanted, even if they couldn't say why.
Lilly noticed first.
She didn't say it right away, but the looks started to shift. Her smiles were thinner. She lingered in the dressing room less. The warmth in her voice cooled, quieted. She stayed in her lane, let Starr orbit in hers.
And that was the first sign something was wrong. Because Lilly had always been steady. Tough. The kind of girl who would throw hands for you in a parking lot without a second thought. The kind who always had gum, and wipes, and a backup pair of lashes in her bag. She was protective, especially with Starr.
But lately, she'd started pulling away.

One night, as they passed each other near the lockers, Starr caught her wrist.

"Everything good?" she asked.

Lilly paused. "Yeah. Just busy."

"Right."

Lilly looked at her for a beat too long. "You sure you're good?"

Starr smiled, bright and fake. "I'm fucking great."

That was the first lie of the night.

It wouldn't be the last.

Aliana was less subtle.

"You're blowing through lines like they're Tic Tacs," she said bluntly one Saturday, arms crossed, eyes sharp as razors.

Starr snorted - literally and metaphorically.

"Everyone does it."

"Not like you."

Starr rolled her eyes. "Don't start."

"I'm not starting. I'm watching." Aliana stepped closer, lowered her voice. "You're slipping, Starr. You're sloppy. You're forgetting which regulars you've already promised dances to. You're leaving your bag open. You're doing rails in the VIP like nobody sees you."

"Maybe I want to be seen," Starr said, voice brittle.

Aliana's mouth twisted. "You think you're invincible right now. But you're not. This club doesn't love you. These people don't love you. They use you."

"I'm using them too."

"That's not the same and you know it."

Starr turned away. "I don't need a lecture."

Aliana didn't follow her. Didn't push.

She just said, "Fine. Don't come crying to me when it all falls apart."

It was around that time Neil stopped showing up on Fridays.

He didn't say goodbye. Didn't ghost her completely either just drifted. Like a balloon slipping from a child's hand. He still came to the club, but now he sat with a newer girl named Dani. A soft-voiced brunette who always looked down when she smiled.

At first, Starr pretended not to notice. But then she did.

And it hurt more than she expected.

Neil had never been hers, not really. But he'd been consistent. Safe. A flickering light in a place built on darkness. He listened to her, back when her words hadn't started slurring. He saw the Charlotte under the Starr.

But the Charlotte was disappearing.

One night, she caught a glimpse of them in the corner Neil and Dani. She walked past their table, letting her hips swing like she didn't care.

But Neil didn't even look up.

And that cut deeper than any slap.

She did another line in the bathroom.

Then another.

And another.

The stall felt like a sanctuary - cold tile, fluorescent light, the hum of bass vibrating the mirror. She stared at herself, breathing hard, pupils wide. Lipstick smudged, glitter clinging to her collarbones. Her eyes looked like glass. Her hands wouldn't stop shaking.

She smiled.

The girl in the mirror didn't smile back.

There were nights she didn't remember leaving the club.

She'd wake up in her apartment with her makeup still on, fingers sticky with glitter, thighs aching, her phone lit up with missed calls she never meant to return. Bags of takeout on the counter, half-eaten. Wine bottles drained. Rolled-up twenties still on the bathroom sink.

Time wasn't linear anymore. It curved, spiraled, collapsed in on itself.

She started showing up to work already high. Not just to feel good, but to feel ready. Ready to perform. To compete. To be the Starr, everyone expected her to be.

She didn't trust herself sober anymore.

The club was louder these days. Or maybe it was just her nerves. Everything buzzed: lights, voices, vibrations from the bass thumping through the

floor. Conversations sounded like static. Faces
blurred together. Everything became movement
and mirrors, a carousel of half-naked bodies
spinning toward nowhere.
But she still danced like a queen.
Still had the room in her palm.
The regulars wanted her. The new money wanted
her. The girls hated her, envied her, mimicked her.
She'd become a myth in real time - Starr with the
legs that never quit, Starr who whispered in your
ear like she knew your darkest secrets, Starr who
made you forget your name for a thousand dollars
an hour.
She became who they needed.
And no one saw the bruises under the highlighter.

Victor showed up on a Wednesday.
Midweek crowd, slow floor, the energy crawling
like a dying animal.
He was the kind of man you'd notice even if you
didn't want to. Mid-forties. Sharp suit. Gold ring.
Watch that probably cost more than most girls
made in a month. He walked with that quiet
entitlement some men wore like a second skin:
rich, used to control, never rushed.
She clocked him from across the room.
It was instinct. Survival. She knew how to spot a
spender. You had to, if you wanted to make real
money.

But Victor didn't act like the others. He didn't wave her over. Didn't toss out hundred-dollar bills like bait. He watched her.

All night.

His gaze was heavy, electric. Not lecherous, but intentional. Like he was memorizing her. Not just how she moved, but who she was beneath it. Like he was reading the parts she hadn't given anyone permission to show.

By midnight, he still hadn't spoken to her.

And that haunted her more than she could explain.

"Who is that?" she asked Valery near the bar.

Valery smirked. "New money. Big money. Word is he just sold something to someone overseas. Oil maybe. Tech. Who cares."

"He hasn't booked anyone?"

"Nope."

Starr's eyes flicked to him again. "Weird."

Valery shrugged. "The quiet ones are the worst."

Starr laughed. "I thought the quiet ones were the best."

Valery raised an eyebrow. "Only if they leave when they're done."

Victor didn't tip that night. Didn't say a word. But when she left at 4 a.m., she found a single red rose on the hood of her car. No note. Just the flower, fresh and fragrant, wet with dew under the streetlight.

She didn't know how to feel about it.

So, she crushed it under her boot.

The drugs kept her moving.

More lines. Faster nights. Shorter skirts. Less of herself in the mirror. She couldn't remember the last time she'd called home. Her mom had texted once: "Just checking in, love you" - but Starr had stared at the message like it was in a foreign language.

Love didn't live here anymore.

Only ambition.

Only cocaine.

Dylan had been watching her too.

More than before.

He liked to flirt, always had, but lately it felt different. More pointed. Like he was testing the waters, waiting for the right moment to make his move.

He caught her by the DJ booth one night, just after she came off stage, breathless and glitter-streaked.

"You know you're gonna kill somebody with that body," he said.

Starr didn't smile. "You practicing your lines again?"

He grinned. "Only for you."

She rolled her eyes, but her lips twitched.

He stepped closer. "You ever think about what it would be like... if you weren't just another girl in here?"

Her eyes narrowed. "What's that supposed to mean?"

He leaned in, his cologne warm and sharp. "It means you're different, Starr. I see that. And maybe I don't want to share you with this place."

"You don't have me," she whispered.

"Not yet."

He let that hang in the air.

She hated how good it made her feel.

And hated herself even more for how much she wanted to believe it.

By now, Lilly barely talked to her.

Aliana was civil, but distant.

Even the floaters stopped asking her for help.

She'd once tried to rescue them, now she was the warning.

And she knew it. Knew her edges were fraying. Her mouth was meaner. Her sleep was worse. She started forgetting songs she used to love. Food had no taste. Sex had no thrill. Her body ached even when she wasn't dancing.

But the money kept coming.

And she kept showing up.

Because what else was there?

Victor wasn't just a customer anymore.

He was a presence.

Some nights she'd catch him before she even saw him, feel his eyes tracking her through the fog of bottle service and bad pop music. He never acted out. Never crossed the line. But he never left, either. And that constant presence started to warp something inside her.

He became a shadow. A rhythm. A whisper in her periphery.

One night, she was sitting backstage, reapplying lip gloss, when she caught his reflection in the dressing room mirror outside the VIP hallway, just standing there, watching.

"What the fuck?" she murmured.

Melody leaned over. "He's always watching you. You didn't notice?"

Starr shrugged, unsettled.

Melody kept going, unfazed. "I heard he comes from money. Like real money. His family owns buildings or some shit. Maybe he's just bored."

"Or dangerous," Starr muttered.

Melody smiled. "Same thing in this place."

The money was better than ever.

There were nights she'd walk out with five grand stuffed in her purse and still feel like it wasn't enough. She couldn't even remember what she was saving for anymore. Freedom? A future? All that felt like a joke now. Her life existed in 15-minute sets, broken up by lines in the bathroom and fake champagne toasts.

She learned to fake moans in VIP, to cry on command for the sweet ones who wanted to "rescue" her. She learned that the house mom always wanted her cut, the DJ favored whoever gave him the biggest tip, and security would look the other way if the price was right.

Charlotte was a ghost now. Starr had taken over. And Starr was expensive.

One night, Dylan cornered her in the hallway outside the private rooms.

"Your set was… intense," he said, leaning in too close.

Starr raised a brow. "That supposed to be a compliment?"

He shrugged. "Take it how you want. You look like you're floating lately."

She didn't respond.

"I mean that in a good way," he added quickly. "Like you're not even trying anymore. You're just… up there. Untouchable."

She stared at him, disinterested. "What do you want, Dylan?"

He leaned in, smirking. "You. Eventually."

Starr exhaled, long and slow. "You should stick to Inga and Melody."

He smiled wider. "Maybe. But they don't make me work for it."

He walked away then, all ego and cologne, and for the first time in weeks, she felt something other than numbness.

Disgust.

And a little bit of fear.

Victor sent her a gift.

Not through the club. Not like the other guys with their roses and jewelry and thinly-veiled expectations. This came to her apartment - no note, no name. Just a black velvet box left on her doorstep.

Inside was a necklace. Thin gold chain. Tiny ruby pendant.

It was beautiful. And "quietly" Expensive.

And it made her stomach drop.

She didn't wear it. Couldn't.

But she didn't throw it away either.

She shoved it into the back of a drawer and tried not to think about what it meant.

The spiral wasn't loud. It wasn't a breakdown, or a screaming match, or some big dramatic collapse.

It was quiet.

It was forgetting to eat. Snorting instead. Missing rent, lying to the landlord. Showing up late to work and sweet-talking Rob into letting it slide. Doing more VIPs than usual. Pushing her body harder. Smiling longer. Pretending better.

Until the pretending felt permanent.

Until she forgot how to turn it off.

One night, the music cut out during her set.

Just silence. Right in the middle of a dance.

The spotlight stayed on her, and for a beat, no one moved.

Then someone laughed. Not cruelly, just drunkenly.

And she stood there, half-naked, heels scuffed, eyes glassy, and felt something inside her cave in. She walked offstage without finishing. The DJ shouted something, but she didn't hear. The club blurred around her.

She ended up on the rooftop.

It was cold. April wind snapping through her hair, slicing across her skin.

She leaned against the railing and looked down at the alley below.

From up here, it all looked so small. The lights, the noise, the bodies. All of it. A stage she didn't want to be on anymore.

She didn't cry. Couldn't.

But her hands were shaking.

Aliana found her there twenty minutes later.

"Jesus, I thought you left," she said, lighting a cigarette.

Starr didn't move.

Aliana took a drag, then handed the cigarette over. Starr took it, her fingers trembling.

"You're not okay," Aliana said.

Starr nodded, just once. "I know."

Silence.

Then Aliana said something soft. Something Starr wasn't ready to hear, but needed anyway.

"You can still leave. Before this place swallows you whole."

Starr didn't answer.

Because the truth was, it already had.

Victor started requesting her by name.

The front desk would whisper it through the earpiece to Rob, and Rob, already tired of the direction things were heading, would find her in the dressing room or bathroom or hallway and say, "Victor's asking."

He never phrased it like an order. Not at first.

She could say no. Technically.

But she didn't.

She'd show up, sit next to him, feel his eyes crawl over her skin like heat, and perform the same story she told every night: a little innocent, a little broken, a little hungry for something.

He liked that version of her. The one who still believed in happy endings.

But she wasn't that girl anymore.

He started staying longer.

Ordering more champagne.

Touching her less but staring harder.

And talking.

God, he talked. About his job in finance. His divorce. His house in Connecticut. His kid who lived with his ex-wife. He talked like she was some sort of mirror he could dump his secrets into and walk away cleaner.

Sometimes he'd pause, tilt his head, and say shit like,
"You're too smart for this place."
She'd laugh, soft and sharp. "So are you."

The club had changed.
Or maybe she had.
The lights felt harsher. The music louder. The customers more handsy, less polite. Everything blurred around the edges now: faces, bodies, cash shoved into G-strings with fingers that lingered too long. Her body moved like a machine, hips rolling to the beat, mind floating somewhere above the stage.
Rob noticed.
He always noticed.
He pulled her aside one night, backstage.
"You good?" he asked.
She was applying lip liner. Her hand didn't even pause. "Peachy."

"Look," he said, quieter now, "you've been off lately. You're slipping."
She kept applying. "Still making money."
"I know. But not everything's about the fucking money."
That caught her off guard. She looked at him.
His eyes were tired. Not angry, just… sad.
"I've seen girls like you," he said. "Too many. You burn bright, then burn out."

She smiled, falsely sweet. "Don't worry about me, Rob. I'm a survivor."
He didn't smile back.

Starr was on autopilot.
She danced. She snorted. She smiled.
She stopped texting Lilly back.
Aliana kept trying, but even she was fading into the background. Melody and Inga were busy playing their own games, especially with Dylan, who seemed to be bouncing between them like a pinball, flashing his smile, testing his charm.
Dylan flirted with her too.
Harder now.
He'd brush past her in the hallway, let his hand trail along her waist. Whisper things. Ask her to stay late. Offer her rides home. Sometimes she'd take them. Not because she wanted to. But because saying no took effort.
He kissed her once, in the car. Out of nowhere.
She didn't kiss back. Just stared at him, too tired to react.
He laughed it off. "You're trouble, you know that?"
She said nothing.

It all went on, until Charlotte passed out in the dressing room.
Nothing dramatic. No seizure or paramedics or anything. Just gone.

She woke up to Valery's voice and the sharp sting of cold water on her cheeks.

"Jesus, Starr. You okay?"

Charlotte sat up slowly, blinking through the haze. Her nose was numb. Her heart racing.

"Yeah. Just tired."

Valery looked skeptical. "You're scaring people."

Starr smirked. "I'm fine. Really."

But she wasn't.

She couldn't remember the last time she ate.

She hadn't called her mom in weeks.

She didn't know what day it was.

And when she looked in the mirror, she barely recognized herself: lashes clumped, glitter smeared, pupils blown wide like two endless holes.

Victor left her a note one night. Handwritten.

"You're not like the others. I see you."

She read it three times.

Then tore it up.

But she didn't throw it away.

She kept the pieces in her locker, like a warning.

Like a secret.

On a Tuesday night, the club was slow.

It always felt more brutal when it was empty, like the place was holding its breath. The music echoing against bare booths. The dancers moving like ghosts. No bachelorettes. No Wall Street wolves. Just stragglers. Regulars. Shadows.

Victor showed up anyway.

Requested her.

She said no.
Rob blinked. "You sure?"
She nodded. "Yeah. I don't want to see him tonight."
Rob didn't ask why. He just nodded and went back to the desk.

Starr sat backstage, wrapped in her robe, staring at the wall. Her hands were shaking again.
Aliana came over, handed her a water bottle. Sat down.
"You gonna talk to me?"
Starr looked at her. "About what?"
Aliana didn't answer. Just waited.
Starr cracked first. "I don't know who I am anymore."
Aliana exhaled. "Then figure it out. Before this place decides for you."
That night, Starr walked home.
The cold bit at her skin. Her heels clicked against the concrete, each step echoing louder than the last. She didn't care. She needed air. She needed to feel something. Anything.

She stopped at a red light, looked up at the city blinking above her.

Bright. Beautiful. Indifferent.

Tears stung her eyes.

Not from sadness. From everything. From nothing.

She wanted to scream. Or disappear. Or start over.

She pulled the ruby necklace from her bag, the one Victor had sent weeks ago. Held it in her palm. It glittered under the streetlight like blood.

She threw it into a storm drain.

Then kept walking.

Chapter 9: Enemies and Egos

The room reeked of sweat, sex, and stale smoke. Charlotte sat on the edge of the hotel bed, elbows on her knees, chin buried in her hands. Her lips were dry. One eyelash had half-peeled off during the night, now drooping like the last thread of dignity. The sun had no business being that bright - it was like God Himself had decided to shame her through the slits in the dusty curtains.

She squinted at the mess on the floor: a pair of lace panties, a spilled bag of cocaine smeared across the nightstand and a Rolex that didn't belong to her. Or maybe it did now.

The man beside her snored with his mouth open, a bloated banker type who'd spent five grand to "feel alive" again. Starr had danced on him like she was performing CPR on a corpse. When she excused herself to the bathroom halfway through, he didn't even notice.

She was used to mornings like this, but they still left a pit in her stomach. The guilt had faded months ago. What was left now was something quieter, emptier - a numb buzz in her chest. The kind of feeling you get after crying too long, when the tears stop but the ache still floats there like smoke.

She slipped her phone out of her purse. Five missed calls from Rob. A text from Dylan: "U up?" - sent at 4:12 a.m. She stared at it. What did he want? What did any of them want?

She didn't answer.

Instead, she grabbed a hundred from the wad of cash on the table and called a cab.

At the club that night, the air was heavier than usual. Like it had absorbed all the secrets from the night before and was now hanging on to them like sweat.

Starr walked in wearing a long coat over a skin-tight dress, her heels clicking in sharp rhythm on the tile. Her face was fresh but blank, a canvas of foundation, contour, and indifference. The dressing room chatter stopped as she entered, just for a second, but it was enough.

Valery glanced at her through the mirror and muttered something under her breath to Anna, who smirked.

Starr peeled off her coat slowly, her back to them, pretending not to notice. But her ears burned. The dressing room used to be her sanctuary, a place of girlish chaos and camaraderie. Now it felt like a war zone. You didn't know who'd pull the trigger, only that someone eventually would.

"Don't forget to thank me for introducing you to Victor," Valery said flatly, applying a thick coat of lip gloss. "He's paying for your rent now, right?"

Starr turned. "He's not paying for anything I didn't earn myself."

Valery scoffed. "Right. You 'earned' it."

Anna joined in, tossing her hair. "You also earned that regular of mine? The one who tipped you a thousand last Friday?"

"He came to me," Starr said, forcing calm into her voice.

Anna stood up. "Because you paraded in front of him like a fucking peacock while I was getting a drink. That's low."

"Girls," Rob said, appearing at the doorway like a weary principal. "Cut the high school shit. Anna, if he switched to Starr, he's not yours anymore. That's the job. Get over it."

Anna sneered but said nothing. Valery stared coldly at Starr in the mirror.

That look stayed with her the rest of the night.

It started with a whisper.

"Did you hear about Carla?"

By midnight, it was a roar.

Carla was one of the newer girls - early twenties, with innocent eyes and a soft Midwestern accent that made customers feel powerful. She wasn't flashy, but she hustled. She laughed at the right times. She batted her lashes and made men feel young again.

But tonight, she'd made a mistake.

Starr was finishing a lap dance when she saw Carla being led through the hallway near the bar by two security guards. Her platform shoes scraped the tile like a protest. Her mascara had already begun to streak, and her voice was rising.

"I didn't take anything! That guy gave it to me!"

"Just come to the office," one of the guards muttered.

"No! I swear to God, I didn't"

The club kept playing music like nothing was happening. Bass thumped. Lights pulsed red. But every girl on the floor saw it. Every man drinking champagne noticed the commotion and tilted their heads, curious. And when Steve himself came down from the office and called Carla a "fucking thief" loud enough for half the VIP section to hear, the club collectively froze.

Carla disappeared into the back, flanked by security.

The whispers started again.

"She took a wallet."

"No, it was a ring. Diamond."

"Some Saudi guy's watch. Rolex."

"Was it Victor's?"

"No. If it was Victor, she'd be dead."

By the time Starr returned to the dressing room, Carla's locker was open. Her belongings had been dumped into a black garbage bag and set by the back door. A few stray lashes clung to the mirror. Her makeup was still scattered across the vanity, left like evidence at a crime scene.

Rob came in and didn't need to raise his voice.

"This place is not a fucking playground," he said. "Anyone caught stealing, even so much as a dollar, will be out. No questions. We've got eyes everywhere. I won't say it again."

He looked around, meeting every girl's gaze. But when he got to Starr, he paused.

There was something in his eyes, not anger.

Worry.

Then he left.

The room was silent for a beat, then Valery chuckled.

"Guess she couldn't keep her hands off other people's shit either."

No one laughed.

But no one defended Carla either.

Starr found out the next day.

Inga had slipped. Or maybe she'd wanted her to know.

They were both on break, sitting behind the club in the alleyway where the girls smoked and whispered between shifts. It was cold, and Starr's coat was too thin, but she stayed out anyway, she needed air. Inga lit a cigarette and said nothing for a while.

Then, casually: "So Dylan's good in bed."

Starr blinked.

She turned her head slowly, like maybe she'd misheard.

"What?"

Inga blew out smoke. "I didn't mean to. It just happened. He came into my room after close last night. Said he was bored."

Starr's heart dropped, but her face didn't flinch. Years of practice.

"Right," she said. "Of course."

"He said he used to like you," Inga went on. "But you got too heavy. Emotionally, I mean. Guys like him they want the fantasy. Not the baggage."

Starr stared at the wall behind the dumpster.

It wasn't the sex that hurt. She didn't even want Dylan, not really. It was what he represented, the last little thread of hope that someone might see her. Not Starr, not the persona. Charlotte.

Gone now.

She nodded, stood up, and went back inside.

Victor started waiting for her.

Not inside, like most men, draped over velvet couches, sipping overpriced bourbon, pretending to be gods. No, he waited outside. By the curb. Across the street. Sometimes near the alley where the dancers smoked. Other times right in front of the door, leaning against a black car with tinted windows and a driver who never looked up from his phone.

He always wore the same thing: dark suit, darker smile.

At first, it was subtle. Flowers left at the bar with her name on the card. A bottle of perfume she hadn't asked for in her locker. A necklace - real diamonds, no note, just waiting on her vanity like a gift from a ghost.

Then it escalated.

He began sending messages through the other girls. "Victor says you looked tired tonight." "Victor wants to take you somewhere quiet." "Victor's asking if you've been avoiding him."

Rob warned her once. Pulled her into his office and sat on the edge of his desk, arms crossed.

"I know he's been... close," he said.

"He's a good customer," Starr replied, keeping her voice flat.

"He's unstable," Rob said. "And he thinks he owns you. You need to set some boundaries."

Starr nodded. She didn't tell Rob about the gift Victor left at her apartment. It had been delivered in a velvet box - a bracelet, antique, expensive. Inside the box was a small note, written in careful, slanted script:

"For the girl who dances like she's trying to forget."

She threw it away, but it didn't matter. That night, Victor waited outside the club again. This time he didn't smile.

The VIP room was velvet-drenched silence, except for the dull thud of bass echoing faintly through the walls. The lights were low, tinged with red. Like blood under water. Like warning signs, she had long ago learned to ignore.

Starr stepped in first, heels clicking against the floor. She forced her posture into that practiced slink: hips loose, shoulders dipped, expression blank and sultry. Her customer followed. A man in his fifties. Greasy gold rings. Tight black shirt stretched over a gut. His cologne was thick, but underneath it, just barely, was something familiar. Sweat. Cigarettes. Old aftershave.

The smell was wrong. Or too right. It dragged something from deep in her memory, sharp and dirty.

Her breath caught in her throat. She smiled anyway. Sat down beside him.

"Hi, baby," she cooed.

He reached for her waist without asking.

That was normal. They all touched like they owned you. But his hands...those hands - were dry and rough in a way that hit her body like static. He squeezed, not gently, and pulled her into his lap like he was rearranging furniture.

"You're softer than you look," he murmured into her ear.

His voice was low. Hoarse. Familiar in a way that had no business being familiar.

She froze for a split second, but then she moved again, automatic, a puppet pulled by strings. She swayed. Rolled her hips. She let her fingertips trail down his chest, like she was still there.

But she wasn't.

Her mind had gone sideways.
It wasn't the man in the club anymore. It was
someone else. Him.
Her brother.

It was his voice in her ear now. His breath against
her cheek. That sick tone he'd used, when he
called her pretty in the hallway, when he told her
to "relax," when he said, "Don't ruin this for us."

The man on the couch groaned softly, gripping her
thigh. She couldn't hear the music anymore. Just
the ringing in her ears. Her stomach flipped.
"You were made for this," he said.
Her whole body seized.
That phrase. Word for word. The exact same thing
her brother had whispered the first time he pulled
her into his room and shut the door.
You were made for this.
The red lights blurred.
Her vision shrank to a pinhole.
A scream clawed its way up her throat but never
made it out.
She tore away from him, stumbling backward,
clutching the edge of the table for balance. The
man reached for her again, annoyed. "What the
hell are you doing?"

She didn't answer. Couldn't.
She yanked her robe from the chair, fumbled to get it on, and backed toward the door.

"I...I need a minute," she choked.
"You haven't finished your time."
But she was already gone.
She ran down the hallway, past the booths and the mirrored walls and the staring bouncers. Past the bar where girls flirted with men too drunk to notice. She reached the private dressing room bathroom, slammed the door, and locked it with shaking hands.
Then she fell to the tile floor.
She didn't cry right away.
First came the trembling. Her arms went numb. Her mouth was dry. She pressed her back against the cabinet under the sink and stared at the grout between the floor tiles like it held the answers to all the questions she'd buried.
How could this still be happening?
How could her body remember something her mind had worked so hard to forget?
A small, helpless sound escaped her lips—like a hiccup, like a sob that hadn't formed yet.
Then the tears came.
They weren't pretty. Nothing about this was.
Her breath stuttered in short, shallow gasps. Her lashes clung together with mascara. Her nose ran. Her hands clawed at her own skin like she could

rip the memory out of her body. She folded forward and pressed her forehead to her knees, rocking slightly, the way she used to as a child when the nights were too long and too quiet.

She was fifteen again.
And he was behind her.
His hand over her mouth. His voice in her ear. His weight on her back.
She'd never screamed. She hadn't known if she was allowed to. The silence of it all had rotted something in her.
And now, here, over a decade later, in a room meant for seduction, it all came back like a flood she couldn't escape.
The bathroom light buzzed softly overhead. She looked up at the mirror.
Her reflection barely registered as human.
Eyes wide and wet, cheeks red and raw, a fake eyelash hanging off her cheek like a broken wing. Lipstick smeared across her chin.
This was Starr. The fantasy. The product.
But underneath, Charlotte was breaking apart again.
She whispered it to herself.
"Not again. Not again. Not again…
But it was. Her body had kept the score. Her body had never forgotten.
She curled tighter into herself, fists clenched, and sobbed until her lungs gave out.

Starr didn't know how long she stayed there.

It could've been five minutes. Could've been an
hour. Time folded in on itself when you were
falling apart.
Eventually, the panic ebbed, slowly, like a tide
pulling back from wreckage. Her sobs turned to
shudders. Her breath found its rhythm again. She
rinsed her face with cold water, watching the
mascara run in streaks down the drain like dirty
ink.
She didn't recognize herself.
Her reflection wasn't Starr. It wasn't Charlotte
either. Just some exhausted shell in a robe,
smeared makeup, and pain leaking from the edges.
She forced herself to stand.
The hallway back to the dressing room felt like a
walk through a war zone. Everything was too
bright. Too loud. The music thumped through the
walls like a heartbeat trying to drag her under.
When she pushed open the dressing room door, a
few heads turned.
Anna looked up from her makeup table, chewing
gum lazily.
"Damn, you look like shit."
Valery didn't say anything, just glanced at her
through the mirror and smirked.
Inga was painting her toenails. Melody was
texting. Jennifer flipped her hair and said, "You
okay?"

Starr nodded.

"Just got too hot in the room," she mumbled.
Everyone went back to what they were doing.
That was how things worked here. You break
down quietly, pull yourself back together even
quieter, and get back on the floor. No one wanted
your darkness. No one had time for your truth.
You learned to wear your trauma like perfume -
undetectable to most, but clinging to you just the
same.
She sat down at her station, hands still trembling,
and reached for a makeup wipe.
Her skin felt raw. Her eyes burned. But she wiped
away the streaks, reapplied her face, and painted
herself pretty again.
Like nothing had happened.
Like she hadn't just relived the worst night of her
life under a man who didn't even know what he'd
done to her.
As she fixed her lashes, Rob peeked into the room.
"Hey," he said, too softly. "You good?"
"Fine," she replied without looking up.
His gaze lingered. He knew something was wrong.
He always did. But this place wasn't built for
saving. It was built for surviving.
"All right," he said finally. "Let me know if you
need a minute."
She didn't answer.
The door closed.

Inga's voice cut through the silence a few minutes later.

"Victor's asking for you again."

Starr's hand froze mid-stroke of eyeliner.

She didn't turn around.

"I'm not taking him tonight."

Inga raised an eyebrow. "He won't like that."

"I don't care."

That earned a smirk. "Sure, you don't."

But Starr didn't respond.

She stared at her reflection instead. At the girl looking back at her.

She wasn't sure if she'd ever get her back.

She left early that night and never saw Victor again…

Slipped out through the back door in jeans and a hoodie, hair shoved under a beanie, face scrubbed clean. No glitter. No lashes. No scent of perfume clinging to her skin.

She walked, even though her feet ached.

The city felt cruel in the early morning. Cold air bit at her cheeks. The streets were half-dead: taxis prowling, garbage trucks growling, streetlights flickering like old ghosts. She passed shuttered storefronts and puddles reflecting neon. She didn't know where she was going. She just needed to move.

She stopped at a diner on Ninth Avenue. One of those old ones with cracked booths and silver napkin dispensers and waitresses who didn't ask questions. She ordered black coffee and toast. The waitress gave her a look but didn't push.

Starr sat in the booth by the window, hands wrapped around the mug, and stared into the dark. Inside her chest, everything felt hollowed out. She thought about that little girl version of herself. The one who used to read under the covers with a flashlight. Who wore her mom's lipstick and danced in front of the mirror. Who thought love was something soft, something that would arrive like a rescue.

That girl was dead.

Buried the night her brother first touched her. And Starr, Starr was what grew in her place. Beautiful. Unbreakable. Untouchable. A fortress of sex and control and perfectly curled hair.

But tonight, the cracks showed.
Tonight, the mirror shattered.
She kept seeing her own face in that VIP room, seeing herself freeze, seeing herself flee, seeing the panic flood through her bones like fire.
She wasn't okay.
Not anymore.
Maybe she never had been.
The coffee went cold in her hands. Outside, the sky began to bleed from black to blue. Morning

was coming. Another shift would follow. Another face to wear.

But for now, in this ugly little booth, she let herself sit in the ruins.

No music. No lights. No one watching.

Just the ache of memory and the silence of survival.

And somewhere inside that silence, a small voice whispered:

You can't keep doing this.

Not like this.

Not forever.

Chapter 10: Crash

The lights didn't dazzle anymore. Not the strobes, not the stage. Not even the glitter smeared across her collarbones. Everything had lost its luster.

Starr moved like a ghost through the floor, hips swaying on autopilot, eyes blank behind thick lashes. She smiled when she had to, flipped her hair like she was taught, leaned in close enough for customers to feel chosen. But she wasn't there. Not really.

After the panic in the VIP room, she'd promised herself she'd take a break. Pull back. Stay clean. But that was a lie. The second she stepped through the doors of the club, the air shifted. The adrenaline kicked in, and her hands twitched for a bump.

Cocaine. That was her reset button.

Upstairs in the dressing room, she chopped quick lines on the mirror behind her makeup kit. A little bump before her set. Another in between dances. Sometimes just to make the mirror version of herself stop looking so much like a stranger.

It helped her forget the voice.

You were made for this.

She hadn't slept in two days. Not really. Just collapsed in short spells with her clothes still on and the TV blaring. Her body was starting to rebel, hands shaky, mouth dry, heart fluttering like a bird in a cage.

But it didn't matter. The show had to go on. Customers didn't care if you were breaking down as long as your lips were glossy and your ass was swaying in their lap. The music was too loud to hear your own heartbeat anyway.

She caught herself zoning out onstage, staring past the lights into the shadows. A man called her name from the edge of the stage and she blinked, snapped back into her body, smiled like she meant it.

Lilly used to catch those moments. She'd lean in during their cigarette breaks and say, "You're not here. Where do you go when you check out like that?"

But Lilly was gone now.

Vanished.

No explanation. No goodbye.

Her locker sat cold and empty beside Starr's, untouched for days. No one said her name out loud, like it would summon something bad.

Inga said she'd heard Lilly took off with some rich guy in Jersey.

Melody said she was back in rehab.

Jennifer said she OD'd and no one was talking.

Starr didn't believe any of it.

She didn't believe anything anymore.

Just the powder on her mirror, the crackle of dollar bills, the rhythmic grind of her body against strangers. She danced because she didn't know what else to do. She danced because it was the only time she could float out of her skin and pretend she was someone else.

But the pretending was starting to crack.

She felt it in her chest. In her teeth. In her dreams, when she had them. Flashes of childhood. Her brother's hand. Her mother's voice. All tangled up in lights and music and men who smelled like cologne and power.

Tonight, the music felt slower.

The lights felt too bright.

She sat at her vanity, eyes rimmed in black, and stared at her reflection as if waiting for it to shatter.

Instead, she reached for her bag. One more bump. Just to level out.

Her nose burned. Her heart kicked. The mirror girl blinked once. Then smiled.

Fake. Fragile.

Just enough to keep going.

The next night, Lilly's locker was still untouched. Her perfume was gone. Her spare lashes. The broken brush with strands of copper hair caught in the bristles. Nothing.

Starr stared at it for a long time before dressing for her shift, her own things spread across the station next to the void. A quiet emptiness now sat where

Lilly used to hum while curling her hair, where she once whispered gossip or handed over lip gloss like it was a sacred offering.

She scrolled through her phone on break, thumb hovering over Lilly's name. She hadn't texted in days. Hadn't called either. They had fought: a dumb, quick, coke-fueled argument about money, something stupid, but it didn't matter anymore. Now it felt like she'd disappeared into smoke.

Starr finally tapped the call button. One ring. Two. Voicemail.

Again.

She tried Melody. "Hey," she asked casually, "have you heard from Lilly?"

Melody didn't look up from her lashes. "Nope. She's probably off with some loser again."

"She wouldn't just vanish," Starr said.

Melody shrugged. "She has before."

Starr didn't answer. Instead, she walked to the front desk and asked Rob.

He glanced up from the clipboard.

"She hasn't shown in five nights," Starr said. "That's not like her."

Rob's face tightened, then softened. "People leave here all the time. Sometimes they come back. Sometimes they don't."

"But you don't think something's happened?"

"She's not your responsibility," he said gently.

"She was my friend."

Rob looked down at the clipboard again. "You can't save everyone here, Starr. You'll drown trying."

That stuck in her chest, heavy and low. She nodded, numb, and walked away.

Later that night, she checked Lilly's Instagram. No stories. No posts. The last one was two weeks ago - a mirror selfie with pink lipstick and a caption that said, "Karma's a mirror, baby."

Starr scrolled the comments. Nothing recent. She opened her texts, reread the last message she'd sent: "Call me back, bitch. I miss you."

It sat there, unanswered.

The club roared on around her. A Friday night, packed wall to wall. The lights blinked like sirens. Laughter, money, slurred flirting. She felt a slow panic build in her chest - irrational, sharp. What if Lilly was dead? What if no one even knew?

No one would say a word. Not here. Not in this world. Girls came and went, vanished like vapor. A new one would be hired next week. Same heels, same hair, same name probably.

They'd call her candy or baby or jade.

And no one would remember Lilly.

Not the way Starr did.

Not the night she pulled Starr's hair back while she puked her first time off coke. Not the way she cried about her dad when she was drunk. Not the way she once said, "You ever think this place is eating us?"

Yes, Starr had thought that. She thought it all the time now.

She shoved her phone deep in her locker, slammed the door, and turned back to the floor. Her next customer was waiting.

The dressing room was unusually quiet.
The kind of quiet that settles over a place before something breaks. Half the girls were still on stage or working the floor. The others were in various stages of undress, sipping Red Bull or retouching mascara. No one spoke much. Everyone was too tired or too wired.

Starr sat at her station, staring into the mirror. She looked like a ghost of herself - foundation too thick, mascara flaking, cheekbones too sharp, eyes glassy and twitching. The cocaine hadn't hit right this time. It made her stomach turn. Her fingers trembled as she reached for her phone, then pulled her hand back.

She'd already texted Lilly again. No response.
She checked her reflection again. Her lips looked pale. Her eyes didn't blink at the right speed. She tried to smile. It looked wrong.
A dull throb started in her temple.

She grabbed her bag and pulled out the small baggie of powder, the one she told herself she'd throw away. Instead, she dumped a line out onto the back of a compact mirror, rolled up a receipt, and inhaled.

Too fast.
Too much.

Her head snapped back from the burn. Her vision blurred. The girls around her blurred too, like reflections in a foggy window. Someone giggled behind her. Music boomed from the stage. The world tilted slightly, like she was on a boat in choppy water.
She wiped her nose and leaned forward, squinting at her reflection.
Still didn't look right.
She felt hot suddenly. Sweat prickled at the back of her neck. Her heart galloped.
It was too much.
She knew it immediately.
But her body didn't care.
The panic came fast, a jagged wave. Her hands started to shake harder. Her jaw clenched involuntarily. She stood up abruptly, knocking over a can of hairspray. No one looked.
She took a step.
Her knees buckled.
The floor came at her in slow motion. The world slowed, narrowed, folded into itself. Her hands couldn't catch her. Her head hit the linoleum hard. Then nothing.

Dark.

And in that dark, a flash.

A door.

A hallway.

A little girl crying.

A man's voice whispering her name.

Starr, wake up.

But that wasn't the voice from the memory.

That was Rob.

His voice sounded like it was underwater.

"Starr, hey. Hey! Starr…shit. Somebody help me!"

Voices now. Louder. Shuffling. A chair scraped.

"Get water, fuck, where's her stuff?"

A slap to her cheek. Her head lolled.

"Starr! Come on. Don't do this to me."

Rob was kneeling beside her. His face swam in and out of focus. His hands on her shoulders, shaking her. Cold water splashed her face. Someone cursed.

"She's burning up," another girl said, voice high-pitched and scared. "She's not breathing right."

"She's breathing. She's breathing," Rob muttered, trying to convince himself. "Come on, come on…"

Another splash of water. Another slap.

"Wake the fuck up, Starr."

She gagged.

A dry heave.

Then a gasp, her lungs clawed for air.

Rob held her head as her whole body shook like a wire strung too tight.

Somewhere in the room, Melody was crying.

A manager burst in, shouting.

"What the hell is happening"

"She overdosed," Rob snapped.

"We can't call anyone. You know that," the manager hissed.

"I don't give a fuck," Rob said. "She could've died."

Starr tried to speak but couldn't. Her throat was sand. Her tongue didn't work.

Her vision blurred again, but she could make out Rob's hand gripping hers.

"You're okay," he whispered. "You're okay."

The next thing she remembered; she was in his car. Lying across the back seat, wrapped in someone's jacket. Her head throbbed. Her mouth tasted like metal. The city moved past the windows in streaks of red and white.

She moaned softly, eyes fluttering.

Rob glanced in the mirror. "Don't try to sit up."

"Where... where are we..."

"You passed out. At work."

"Did I..."

"You're okay now," he said, quieter. "You're gonna be okay."

He didn't take her to a hospital.

He took her to his apartment.

She didn't protest.

His place was small. Clean. Sparse. She'd never seen it before. He helped her inside like she was made of glass, guiding her to the couch and wrapping her in a blanket.

"Drink this." He handed her a glass of water.

Her hand shook too much to hold it.

He helped her sip.

She felt like a child. Humiliated. Exposed. But alive.

And that counted for something.

He sat on the floor next to her. For a long time, neither of them spoke.

"I thought you were gone," he said finally. "You were cold. You weren't breathing right."

"I didn't mean to," she whispered.

"I know."

"I just wanted to feel… okay."

Rob didn't answer. His jaw clenched. His eyes were red.

"Where's Lilly?" she asked after a long silence.

He looked at her. "I don't know."

"She's not answering."

"I know."

"I think she's really gone this time."

Rob exhaled, long and slow. "People disappear when they're in pain. Some come back. Some don't."

Starr looked down at her hands.

They didn't feel like hers anymore.

"I used to think this was just a phase," she said. "The dancing. The coke. The… everything. I thought I'd wake up one day and be back in my old life. But that life's gone."

He didn't interrupt.

"I don't know who I am anymore."

"You're alive," he said.

"That's not enough."

"It has to be. For now."

Tears welled in her eyes.

She didn't wipe them away.

He didn't try to fix her.

He just sat with her in the quiet.

Later, he let her sleep in his bed while he took the couch. She curled under the covers, shaking despite the warmth. The night crawled past slowly, each minute soaked in guilt, fear, and something else, something hollow and unfamiliar.

She wasn't invincible.

She wasn't untouchable.

She'd danced too close to the edge, and it had grabbed her by the throat.

Tomorrow, she would have to go back to the club. Back to the mirrors, the money, the lies. Back to pretending. But for tonight, she let herself feel the truth:

She almost died.

And no one but Rob noticed.

Not the girls. Not the managers. Not the
customers. Not even Lilly.
She stared at the ceiling for hours, afraid to close
her eyes.
Because in the dark, she kept seeing that little girl.
The one who used to believe in escape.

The club didn't say a word.
No memo. No meeting. No whisper of what
happened in the dressing room.
It was as if it hadn't happened at all.
Starr showed up the next night, bruised inside and
out. Rob had begged her to take a few days off,
but she shook her head.
"If I stop now," she'd said, "I won't come back."
And she wasn't ready to leave.
Not yet.
So, she walked back in like nothing had happened.
Hair curled. Lashes thick. A new tube of red
lipstick smeared across lips that still felt numb.
The other girls barely looked at her, except for
Melody, who gave her a long, strange stare, then
turned away.

No one asked if she was okay.
Maybe they didn't care.
Maybe they were scared of what she'd say.

Or maybe they knew if they acknowledged her collapse, they'd have to look at their own.

So, the music played on. The stage called.

Customers kept coming.

Everything looked the same.

But something inside Starr had cracked.

She didn't feel like a star anymore. She felt like a warning.

She kept glancing at the corner of the dressing room where it happened, where her body hit the floor and no one noticed until Rob stormed in. She touched the edge of the vanity where her compact had spilled. Where the powder had turned to poison.

She hadn't touched coke since that night.

Her body still ached for it. Her hands still twitched. But the thought of that cold tile floor, of Rob's voice shouting her name, of the cold grip of death sneaking up her spine, it was stronger than the high.

For now.

She danced slower. She smiled less. She didn't fake it as well.

But she showed up.

That was all she could do.

One night, after her shift, she lingered at the front bar. Rob was closing tabs, wiping counters. She didn't speak. Just watched him, the way he carried himself: solid, calm, real.

He noticed her finally and walked over.

"You shouldn't be here late."

"I couldn't sleep."

"You haven't been using?"

She shook her head. "I want to. But I haven't."

He studied her, as if trying to believe her. Then nodded once.

"I'm proud of you," he said, soft.

She looked down.

"You saved me."

"You saved yourself. I just got in the way."

"No," she said. "You pulled me back."

Silence stretched between them, heavy but warm.

"I don't know how to be okay," she whispered. "But I'm starting to see how close I came to disappearing."

"You didn't," he said. "You're still here."

Starr nodded.

Maybe that was the beginning.

Not healing.

Not redemption.

Just staying.

Just not vanishing.

Starr stood in front of the dressing room mirror, face bare, hair undone. It was late, almost morning. The club had emptied, the music silenced, the floor cleaned and mopped. Only the ghosts remained now, drifting in the corners, whispering between hangers and half-empty glasses.

She studied her reflection.

Not the costume.

Not the hair or the shoes or the pose she'd perfected.

Just her.

The hollows under her eyes. The faint yellowing bruise on her collarbone. The tiny red capillaries in the whites of her eyes from crying too much, or from not sleeping, or both.

And deeper than that, something she hadn't seen in a long time.

The girl from before.

Before New York. Before the club. Before the dressing room floor swallowed her.

She didn't look innocent.

She didn't look saved.

But she looked alive.

And that mattered.

Behind her, the room was silent. No voices. No music. No Lilly. No Valery or Anna. No threats. No claws. No customers pushing hundreds into her hands like they owned her.

Just Starr.

Just Charlotte.

She took off her heels slowly. Her feet throbbed from hours of standing. The red indents around her toes marked the cost of survival.

She peeled off her lashes next.
One by one.
Then wiped the red lipstick off her mouth,
revealing the curve of her real lips, no longer
coated in someone else's desire.
She thought of Lilly, still gone. Thought of
Victor's hands in the VIP room. Thought of
Dylan's smirk. Thought of Rob pulling her back
from the dark.
She touched the mirror gently.
Her fingers left a smear on the glass.
A trace of reality.
Not sparkle. Not seduction. Not performance.
Just her.
And the crack inside her that was beginning to
split wide open.
Because no one tells you that the glitter cuts. That
the money makes you hungry and empty at the
same time. That once you sell a version of
yourself, it's hard to remember what the original
looked like.
She didn't know what came next.
She just knew she couldn't go back.
The coke. The collapse. The silence afterward.

It all meant something now.
Something louder than the music.
She turned away from the mirror and gathered her
things.

As she walked out of the dressing room for the night, she left the costume behind. The dress. The lashes. The heels.

She stepped into the early morning air barefoot.

It was cold.

It was real.

It didn't ask her to smile.

And for the first time in a long time, she didn't feel like she had to.

Chapter 11: The Machine

The club didn't glow anymore.

It buzzed, it pulsed, it fed, but the glow was gone. Starr stood outside under the red awning, looking up at the neon sign like it was a cage on fire. The same bouncers nodded. The same perfume-sick air leaked out the door. Same music throbbed from inside.

But she wasn't the same.

She stepped inside anyway.

Her heels clicked on the floor as she walked past the coat check, past the velvet ropes, into the belly of it all. The lights hit her like judgment, pink and gold and blue, slicing her open. She forced a smile for the host, who didn't notice the stiffness in it. The place hadn't changed. But it felt different. Everything did.

She walked past the bar, catching Rob's eye. He nodded once. No smile. No warmth. He was colder now - guarded. Ever since he carried her to his apartment that night, something had shifted between them. He didn't ask how she was. He didn't touch her. He let her move through the club like a ghost with a name.

She didn't blame him.

He'd saved her life, and now she was back in the fire.

The girls in the dressing room looked up briefly, then went back to their own reflections. Melody gave a half-hearted smile. Anna said nothing. Valery didn't even turn around.

No one mentioned her fall.

That was the rule: act like survival is a skill, not a fluke.

Starr sat down and began to paint her face.

But she wasn't dressing up to shine anymore.

She was armoring up to endure.

Out on the floor, the customers were the same. Hungry smiles, eyes that wanted to devour. Men with wallets full of reasons to forget who they were. But now, every time they reached for her, Starr saw the machine behind it. How everything fed on everything else.

The club chewed girls like her and spat them out as memory.

She danced anyway.

She danced because she didn't know what else to do.

Dylan walked back into the club like it belonged to him.

Because it did.

Not legally, his father still held the deed, but in all the ways that mattered, Dylan was the crowned prince of that place. The way the bouncers stepped aside without a word. The way the bartenders poured before he ordered. The way the dancers' eyes lit up or narrowed, when they saw him.

He strolled in wearing black. Black dress shirt, black jeans, no tie. His hair longer than before, curled behind his ears like he didn't give a damn, like he hadn't just disappeared for weeks. He wore his arrogance like cologne - thick, intoxicating, and just shy of offensive.
Starr saw him from across the floor.
It was late, past 2 a.m., when the club thinned and the music softened to a darker, slower beat. She was leaning against the back bar, her stilettos killing her, watching Anna hustle some finance guy near the rail. And then, just like that, he appeared.
He hadn't changed.
And she hated how her stomach flipped anyway.
He didn't look at her right away. He took his time. Ordered a drink, said something charming to one of the new girls, dark hair, too much highlighter on her cheekbones, looked maybe nineteen. The girl giggled.
Starr turned away. She didn't want to be pulled in. Not again. Not now, with the machine breathing down her back and her own blood still warming from the cold floor.
But Dylan was gravity.

And she'd always had weak knees.

When he finally crossed the room to her, it was like watching a wave come in - smooth, inevitable. "Starr," he said.

His voice was silk dipped in smoke. Familiar. Dangerous.

"Dylan," she replied, cool as she could manage. "Didn't know you were back."

"I heard about what happened," he said, leaning in just enough that she could smell the expensive bourbon on his breath. "You okay?"

She blinked. "Fine."

He didn't push. Just nodded, letting silence work its magic.

"I missed your shows," he said. "Still the best one here?"

"I'm the only one still standing," she said flatly.

He smiled at that wide, white, too perfect. "I like a woman who survives."

There was something in the way he said it that made her skin tighten. Like survival was a trick. A dance. A test you passed to be his next obsession.

She turned to leave. "I have a table."

"I'll walk you."

"No need."

He fell into step beside her anyway.

He followed her to a corner table near the back, one of those plush leather booths where the lights dipped low and everything felt a little more dangerous. A man in a suit was waiting: mid-fifties, Rolex, nervous hands. Starr slid into the booth with the practiced grace of a girl who'd learned how to read men before they opened their mouths.

Dylan didn't leave.

He leaned on the partition like he owned the air. The customer looked at him, unsure.

"She's busy," Dylan said smoothly. "Give her a minute."

The man hesitated. Then stood and walked toward the bar, probably to throw money at another girl.

Starr stared at Dylan, eyes narrowing. "That was my table."

"I'll tip you double," he said.

She laughed, bitter and soft. "You think I'm still chasing tips from you?"

"I think you still like to play."

His eyes scanned her face. Not hungrily. Not like the other men. His gaze was slower, sharper, peeling her open in a way that made her want to run and scream and stay, all at once.

"You used to smile when I came around," he said.

"I used to think you meant something."

He didn't flinch. He liked the challenge. Dylan always liked when girls came in strong, because he believed they'd break harder.

"You know what I think?" he said, voice low now. "I think you're tired of pretending none of this touches you."

"It touches everyone."

"But it leaves marks on you," he said. "Pretty ones."

Starr felt her pulse betray her. There was something unbearable in the way he talked to her, like she was a poem no one else had learned how to read.

But she couldn't trust that. Not anymore.

Behind him, Inga hovered.

She'd been watching since he walked in. Her lean body stiff, lips tight. She stood near the DJ booth, pretending to laugh with a bottle girl, but her eyes were locked on Dylan.

She still wore his scent possessively, desperately. She was still his, even if he had stopped noticing.

Inga didn't smile when Starr caught her gaze. Instead, she turned sharply and disappeared down the hall toward the VIP wing.

Dylan noticed. His jaw tightened a fraction.

"She still thinks she's yours," Starr said.

"She's not."

"Does she know that?"

He shrugged. "We were never anything serious."

Starr leaned back against the seat, crossing her arms. "She doesn't look like she got the memo."

"She'll be fine."

But something in his voice betrayed a crack.

That was the thing with Dylan: everything he said was coated in charm. But if you listened close, you could hear the ghosts under it.

He slid into the booth beside her, uninvited.

She didn't move.

"I'm not who I was before," she said, eyes fixed on the stage. "If you're looking for the girl who used to flirt with you between lap dances and Coke bumps, she's dead."

"I'm not looking for a girl," he said. "I'm looking at a woman."

His words landed heavy. Too direct. Too perfect. And Starr hated how part of her wanted to believe him.

Because Dylan wasn't like the other men.

He didn't shove cash at her and expect a moan. He didn't grope. He didn't leer. He watched. He studied. He waited.

He made you want to offer yourself and then forgot your name.

But tonight, something was different.

He wasn't leaving.

He stayed in that booth through her next two rotations. Bought her water, not booze. Listened. Asked questions no one else bothered with.

And Starr: tired, guarded, aching - answered them. Not all the way.

But enough to feel the walls shift.

Backstage, the dressing room was a hive of broken wings.

Inga sat at her station, elbows on the counter, face pale beneath layers of glitter and bronzer. She hadn't spoken to anyone all night. Her lips moved sometimes, silently, like she was reciting some internal prayer or curse.

Starr passed behind her without speaking, but Inga's eyes flicked up to meet hers in the mirror. "You think you're better than me now?" Inga said suddenly.

The words were sharp, but her voice trembled. Starr stopped.

"I don't think about you at all," she said.

Inga stood up. She was tall, fierce in heels, but her body looked thinner now fragile, stretched too tight. Her arms folded across her midsection like she was protecting something.

"You think I don't see how he looks at you?" she hissed. "Like I never existed."

Starr met her eyes. "Maybe stop pretending he ever loved you."

That landed hard. Inga flinched, lips twitching. Then she whispered: "I'm pregnant."

The words punched the air out of the room.

Starr blinked. "You're what?"

"Two months," Inga said. Her voice cracked, but her chin stayed high. "It's his."

Starr took a slow step back, instinctively. "Does he know?"

Inga laughed: bitter, hollow. "He doesn't care."

A long silence stretched between them, thick and full of ghosts.

"He said it wasn't his problem," Inga added. "Said I should 'handle it.'"

Starr felt something inside her shift. Not sympathy. Not yet. But an old, raw ache. That ache of being dismissed, discarded, invisible after you've given everything.

Inga's eyes shone now, glossed with tears she wouldn't let fall. "You think he's different with you? You think you're special?"

Starr didn't answer.

Because part of her wanted to believe she was.

And that part was dangerous.

"Don't make the same mistake I did," Inga said quietly. "Don't fall for him."

She walked out before Starr could respond: long legs trembling under the weight of everything she hadn't said.

Later that night, Dylan found Starr again.

She was sitting in the back hallway, barefoot, legs stretched out on the cold tile floor. The music was muffled here. The air smelled like sweat and dry shampoo.

He crouched down beside her. "You okay?"

She didn't look at him. "Inga told me."

He sighed. "Of course she did."

"You're not even surprised."

"I knew she'd try to use it."

Starr turned to him, anger sparking now. "Use it?"

"She's not keeping it," he said flatly. "She'll get rid of it. She always makes drama out of nothing."

"She's carrying your kid."

"She's unstable," he said. "You've seen it."

"And you think that gives you the right to ignore her?"

His jaw tightened. "What do you want me to do, Starr? Marry her? She's been clinging to me for months."

"She's not clinging," Starr said. "She's drowning."

Dylan didn't answer.

He just stared at her with that same cool expression - calculated, calm, hollow in all the right ways. The kind of emptiness that made people want to fill it.

Starr stood up slowly.

"I'm not going to be your next ghost," she said.

He smiled, but it didn't reach his eyes. "Then don't disappear."

The call came in just after sunrise.

Starr was still in bed, not asleep - just lying there, staring at the ceiling fan, watching the blades spin like a slow clock that would never tell her anything useful.

Her phone buzzed against the cracked screen on her nightstand. She saw the caller ID - Rob, and felt her stomach drop before she answered.

He didn't waste time.

"Inga's dead."

Silence.

The room seemed to hold its breath with her.

"She drowned," Rob said. "In Dylan's pool."

Words dissolved inside her.

"What?" she whispered.

"Police think she jumped in sometime around 4 a.m. No clothes. No note. Nothing."

Starr sat up, the sheet tangled around her legs. Her throat was dry as ash.

"Was she alone?"

"She was living there," Rob said, voice hard now. "Didn't you know that?"

No. She hadn't.

"I thought he kicked her out," she said.

"He did. But she kept coming back. I guess last night was the last time."

The line buzzed softly between them.

"She's gone, Starr," Rob said. "I thought you'd want to know before you came in."

She didn't go in.

She couldn't.

Instead, she pulled the curtains shut, locked her front door, and lay back down with her heart thudding in her chest like a fist trying to get out.

But there was no getting out.

Not now.

By nightfall, the news had spread like spilled champagne on a mirrored floor - quick, cold, and sticky.

The club was quieter than usual. No one said her name out loud, but it was everywhere: on the girls' faces, in the DJ's slower setlist, in the way customers were gently steered away from certain topics.

Anna was the first to say it out loud, in the dressing room, in front of the mirror where Inga used to sit.

"She was always dramatic," she muttered, blotting her lipstick. "I guess she needed the final scene."

No one responded.

Valery lit a cigarette even though it was against the rules. Smoke curled toward the ceiling like a funeral veil.

"She was hurting," Starr said, voice low.

"She was weak," Valery replied, flat. "Weak doesn't last long in this place."

Starr looked at her, really looked. The sharp contour of Valery's cheekbones, the tightness around her eyes. She was scared, too, but she'd rather choke on cruelty than admit it.

No one wanted to admit they'd seen Inga unraveling.

They'd all watched it.

They'd all looked away.

Even Starr.

Especially Starr.

When Dylan arrived, everything went colder.

He walked through the door like nothing had happened. White T-shirt, gold chain, perfect hair. He nodded at the bouncers, fist-bumped the DJ, even flirted with one of the new girls on his way to the back.

Starr was on her way to the locker room when she saw him.

She froze. He stopped, too.

Their eyes met.

He looked… untouched.

"How are you here?" she asked.

"Where else would I be?"

Starr's mouth opened, then closed.

"She was living in your house," she said. "She died in your pool."

"She broke in," he replied, like it was a minor inconvenience. "I wasn't home. It's not my fault."

Starr's blood ran cold.

"She was pregnant."

"She was unstable," Dylan said, voice harder now. "She told everyone she was pregnant. I never saw proof."

"You left her there," she whispered.

Dylan's mouth twisted into something close to a smile, but it didn't have any warmth in it. Just defense.

"I didn't kill her, Starr. She made a choice. That's what people do in this world. They choose."

"No," she said. "She begged."

His face froze.

"I saw her," Starr continued, voice breaking. "She begged you."

Dylan didn't say anything.

He turned and walked away.

Later, Starr stood outside on the back loading
dock, wrapped in her fur-lined hoodie, the night
pressing in like a bruise. Her cigarette trembled
between her fingers. She wasn't crying.
She was just… empty.
The kind of empty that makes you afraid to go to
sleep.
She pictured Inga's body, floating in the pool,
limbs slack, hair drifting like dark seaweed. She
wondered what Inga had been thinking in the final
moment. Whether it had been rage or relief.
Whether she had hoped someone would stop her,
or if the silence was the only thing she'd wanted.
Inga had always loved the water. She used to say it
made her feel clean.
Starr remembered laughing with her once,
barefoot on the edge of a hotel tub, snorting lines
off the porcelain while their feet got wet.
"We're just glitter in the drain," Inga had said.
And maybe that was true.
Maybe they all were.

Two days later, Starr found herself in front of
Dylan's house.
She didn't remember deciding to come
She only remembered waking up to silence, no
music, no sirens, no voice inside her telling her to

move. Just the static hum of her thoughts and the pull of unfinished grief.

The house was too big for the block, all white stone and dark windows behind a wrought iron gate. The kind of place built to keep things out or keep people in.

She buzzed the intercom, expecting no answer.

But the gate clicked open.

No voice. Just a hum and then silence.

She walked in.

The pool was still.

Perfect blue. Chlorine and sky, reflecting nothing.

It was quiet in the backyard, eerily quiet. No music, no laughter, no life.

Starr stood at the edge of the water, staring into it. The sun had passed overhead, and shadows fell across the tile in long strips.

Here. Right here. This was where Inga had floated. Her body had been found face-down. The water had been cool, the police report said. Her lungs had been full. There was no struggle. No sign of hesitation.

She'd walked right in.

Starr crouched and touched the surface of the pool. It was cold. A ripple shivered away from her finger.

She closed her eyes and imagined Inga's final steps.

No note. No scream. Just the soft splash of skin slipping into water. Maybe she hadn't wanted to die. Maybe she just wanted to disappear.

Maybe it was the same thing.

The back door opened behind her.

She didn't turn around.

"Why are you here?" Dylan asked.

Starr stood slowly.

"I wanted to see," she said. "Where it happened."

He lit a cigarette. "Morbid."

"She called me," Starr said.

He blinked. "When?"

"An hour before," she lied. "She left a message."

There was no message. Just a hunch. A need to hurt him with something he couldn't control.

Dylan looked away, jaw tightening. "She had problems. You know that."

"We all have problems."

"She didn't want to be saved."

"Did you even try?"

Dylan exhaled smoke, turning his head so it didn't hit her.

Starr walked past him, toward the door.

"Maybe you should empty the pool," she said.

He didn't answer.

That night, Starr dreamed of water.

She was back at the club, dancing on stage, but the room was flooded. Men sat at the edge of the runway, smoking under the surface, bubbles rising from their mouths as they watched her. Their faces were smooth, pale, featureless like porcelain masks. She moved in slow motion, her hair floating around her like seaweed.

In the corner of the VIP room, Inga stood waist-deep in water, holding out her arms.

"You didn't stop me," she said.

Starr tried to scream, but no sound came.

"You were the only one who saw me," Inga whispered. "And you still let me go."

Then her eyes rolled back, and she sank - slow, beautiful, vanishing like a coin into a wishing well.

Starr woke up gasping, her sheets soaked with sweat, her hands clawing at the air.

The club moved on.

It always did.

Girls went back to work. Music played. Laughter returned, loud and strained. Customers asked about Inga in hushed voices, and then, a week later, stopped asking at all.

The couch in the dressing room where she used to sit was taken by a new girl with too much glitter on her eyelids and bruises on her thighs. No one told her what happened. No one warned her.

The club didn't stop. It absorbed.

It digested.

Starr started skipping her shifts more. Sleeping more. Dreaming more.

In the dreams, Inga came back wet, cold, and silent. She'd sit on the edge of Starr's bed, leaving puddles that didn't dry, her skin pale and bloated, her eyes unreadable.
Sometimes she smiled.

Sometimes she cried.
Sometimes she said nothing at all.
Starr started sleeping with the lights on.

Dylan showed up again two nights later. He found her in the hallway, slipping on her heels.
He leaned against the wall like a confession.
"You look tired," he said.
She didn't answer.
"You know, I think she hated you in the end," he added softly.
She turned.
He smiled: charming, cold, calculated.
"I think she saw the way I looked at you," he continued. "She saw something coming. She always did have good instincts."
"Don't," Starr said.
The hallway stretched longer than it should have, like the whole place had tilted into some surreal nightmare. The walls pulsed with the bass of a song she couldn't hear. Girls passed her like ghosts, lips moving, eyes blank.
She made it to the dressing room and locked herself inside.

For the first time in weeks, she cried.
Not just tears.
She sobbed: deep, primal, broken sobs that
scraped her ribs and shook her bones.

After that, something in her went quiet.
Not dead.
Just quiet.
Like a switch flipped. Like the lights were still on,
but nobody was home.
She did her shifts. She smiled when she had to.
She danced, she flirted, she did the job. But her
eyes were somewhere else, always floating a few
inches above the scene, watching it all with that
hollow, waterlogged detachment.
She stopped using. Not out of virtue. Just…
fatigue.
Even the drugs felt like a performance now.
Even the pain.
A week after the funeral - closed casket, no
family, cheap flowers, Starr went back to Dylan's
house.
She didn't tell anyone.
She didn't know why she was there.
She sat beside the pool again, the water still and
perfect.
She stared into it until the edges blurred.
She thought about stepping in.
Just her toes.
Just to feel what Inga had felt.

She imagined the cold on her skin, the weightlessness, the silence pressing against her eardrums.

Would it feel like flying?

Or falling?

She leaned forward, her fingers skimming the surface.

Inga's voice came back to her, soft and far away: "We're just glitter in the drain."

The words rippled through her.

She stood and walked away.

She wasn't ready to drown.

Not yet.

It started with a rose on her vanity.

Nothing else, just the flower, long-stemmed and blood red, laid across the mirror under the bright glare of the dressing room lights. No card. No note. Just the thorns intact and the scent still heavy from cold air.

Starr stared at it for a long moment before picking it up.

"From your little prince?" Valery said behind her, sauntering past with a smirk. "Or maybe the ghost of Inga, trying to warn you?"

Starr didn't answer. She set the rose aside, careful not to prick her fingers.

That night, Dylan was waiting outside the club in his black car, smoking with the windows down.

He didn't say a word when she climbed in. He just

reached over and pushed a paper bag into her lap, inside: a pair of leather gloves, pale pink, soft as butter.

"You don't like flowers," he said. "Too obvious."

She looked at the gloves.

"You think this is better?"

He shrugged. "You'll wear them longer."

She put them on. They fit perfectly. Warm. Delicate.

He smiled like he'd already won.

He came back every night.

Never inside the club, he didn't like the mess, he said. The smell of desperation in the walls. But he waited for her out front. Bought her little things: a book of poems she'd once mentioned, a necklace too expensive for someone who hadn't even kissed her yet.

Some of the girls started noticing.

"You're next," Anna whispered with a crooked grin. "He always picks one. Then breaks them."

"I'm not interested," Starr lied.

"Doesn't matter," Anna said. "You think Inga wanted him? Look where she is now."

Starr didn't answer.

But the seed was already planted.

One night, she let him take her to his penthouse. She told herself it didn't mean anything. Just curiosity. Just control.

The elevator opened directly into his living room: white walls, dark floors, windows that looked out on the city like it was a painting hung just for him. The space smelled of tobacco and cedarwood. Too clean. Too empty.

He poured her a drink without asking. Sat down across from her like he'd been waiting years to do it.

"You look tired," he said again.

"You already said that."

He smirked. "Still true."

They drank in silence. He didn't try to touch her. He didn't ask about her shifts, her past, her scars. Instead, he said, "I used to sleepwalk."

She blinked. "What?"

"When I was a kid. I'd get up in the middle of the night and walk down to the pool. My father found me once standing at the edge, eyes open, about to jump in. Said I looked peaceful."

She stared at him.

He took another sip. "Sometimes I wonder if I ever woke up."

There was something fragile in his voice, like the stem of the rose.

She didn't trust it.

But she couldn't look away either.

He took her out onto the terrace.

It was massive: larger than the apartments she'd grown up in. Slate floors, glass railing, potted plants that were probably cared for by someone else. The city lay below them like a beast, glittering and hungry.

"I like to come out here when I can't sleep," Dylan said, leaning against the railing. "You can't hear the sirens from up here. Just the wind."

Starr stepped to the edge.

It wasn't fear she felt looking down, it was longing.

He watched her, eyes unreadable. "Do you ever feel like flying?"

"All the time," she said. "But I'm not sure I'd land."

He laughed, but it wasn't warm. "I don't think you're meant to."

She turned to him. "Is that what you thought about Inga?"

His expression didn't change. Not right away. But something in the set of his mouth tightened.

"Inga was... delicate," he said finally. "Too delicate for this place. She cracked."

"You dropped her," Starr said softly.

He looked at her.

"You knew she was pregnant."

"Yes."

"And you still left her."

"She thought it would change things," he said. "It wouldn't have. It never does."

His honesty was brutal. Too smooth. Too clean.
"You're a monster," she said.
He didn't argue.
He just stepped closer, the wind catching his coat.
"I never lied to you," he said.
"You didn't have to."
Their faces were inches apart now. The lights
behind them made his eyes look colder than usual.
"You think you're different from her," he said.
"But you're not. Not really. You're just not broken
yet."
She almost slapped him again.
Almost.
But instead, she kissed him.
Not out of love.
Not even lust.
Out of rage. Out of confusion. Out of that quiet,
aching place inside her that needed to prove she
was still alive.
His lips were soft. His hands stayed at his sides.
When she pulled away, she saw something flicker
in his expression - surprise? Vulnerability? Or just
satisfaction?
She didn't care.
She walked past him, back into the penthouse,
back into her armor.

She didn't see him for two nights.
She thought she'd feel relief.
Instead, she couldn't stop shaking.

Her body didn't trust her anymore. Her reflection didn't look right in the mirror.

In the dressing room, Anna watched her through the reflection.

"So, how's Prince Charming?" she asked.

Starr didn't answer.

"You know," Anna continued, "he gave Inga a rose too. Just one. Same color."

Starr froze.

She reached into her bag later, fingers brushing something cold and soft - another rose.

No note.

Just thorns.

The third rose showed up a week later.

It was left on her fire escape this time, pressed between the iron bars and the frost-stained glass.

She hadn't told Dylan where she lived. Not exactly. But he knew.

Of course he knew.

She stood there barefoot in the cold, the city screaming below her, the wind biting her skin, and stared at it. The petals were darker this time, nearly black at the edges, like they'd burned in some quiet fire before being laid at her feet.

She didn't bring it inside.

She left it there to rot.

By Friday, her stomach turned every time she passed the mirrors in the club. Her makeup felt too bright, her skin too exposed. The lights made her feel like prey. Eyes followed her, hands reached, voices blurred.

"Smile more, sweetheart."

"Come sit with me."

"Where's that fire you used to have?"

She couldn't tell if they were customers or ghosts. She barely recognized herself.

And Dylan, he didn't come inside. Not anymore. But his presence hovered like perfume. People whispered when she walked by. Some girls stared. Others avoided her entirely.

Lola had stopped calling.

Even Valery was quiet now.

There was a hollow forming in Starr's chest, like something was being carved out piece by piece. Slowly. Gently. Like someone rearranging her organs while she slept.

That night, she left early.

She told Rob she had a migraine. He didn't ask questions. He just gave her that same heavy-lidded look, the one that said he knew, but couldn't stop her.

She walked until her heels blistered, then took them off and kept going barefoot. Through puddles. Past neon. Past strangers with eyes like glass.

Eventually she ended up back at Dylan's building. She didn't buzz.

She just looked up at the top floor, at the single light still on.
And somehow, she knew he was watching her.
She felt it like a wire pulling taut in her chest.
When the door opened, she didn't flinch.

The elevator was waiting for her.
Empty.

Silent.
She stepped in and pressed the top floor.
Her reflection in the steel walls looked like someone else, like a woman who had stopped believing in her own story.
Dylan opened the door before she knocked.
He didn't say a word.
Just stepped aside to let her in.
The penthouse was colder tonight. More shadows. More silence. He poured her a drink again. No ice. No smile.
"You're here," he said.
Starr sat down, crossing her legs even though her knees felt like paper.
"I wanted to see the roof again."
He watched her for a long time.
Then nodded once.

The rooftop was darker than before.
No moon. Just the city: lit up like it didn't know how to sleep. Lights flickered in the windows of

the buildings across the skyline like distant warning signs. Somewhere far away, a siren wailed and cut off.

Dylan lit a cigarette and handed it to her.

She took it with shaking fingers.

"You're not what I expected," he said.

"Neither are you."

He leaned against the railing.

"Why did you come here?" he asked.

She walked to the edge and leaned forward just enough to feel the wind lift her hair. The air was sharp. Real. It bit her cheeks and stung her eyes.

"I came here," she whispered, "to remember what falling feels like."

Dylan stepped closer. Not touching. Just near enough that she felt the heat of him again.

"I won't catch you," he said.

She looked at him. "I know."

Then she kissed him again.

And this time, she felt nothing.

They didn't sleep.

They didn't speak.

She laid beside him in the endless white of his bed, the sheets cold despite their bodies, and listened to the silence. Dylan slept like a child: arms loose, mouth slightly parted, like he'd never broken a thing in his life.

She stared at the ceiling and counted the cracks.

There were none.

Of course there weren't.

Everything in his world was flawless, sterile, designed to erase the memory of blood and mistakes. But Starr was all cracks. All fragments. She didn't belong here. She never had.

Her skin itched where his fingers had touched her. The kiss still clung to her like someone else's perfume.

She slipped out of Dylan's bed at dawn.

He didn't stir.

She didn't leave a note. Didn't take the gloves. Didn't look back.

The elevator ride down felt longer than the one up. She watched her reflection in the mirror-paneled walls and thought: This is how ghosts are made. Outside, the sky was the color of concrete and ash. The streets were empty, except for the usual wanderers, the ones who didn't belong anywhere, the ones who looked like she felt.

She walked until her feet blistered again. Until the city softened around her. Until the club felt like a memory and Dylan like a fever dream.

She ended up at the river.

Not because she meant to.

Just because it was there.

The water was slow and black and barely moved. The wind came off it in long sighs. She stood at the railing and closed her eyes.

If she leaned far enough forward, she could imagine it pulling her in. Just like Inga. Just like sleep.

But then something inside her shifted.

It was small.

Barely there.

Like the flutter of a moth against glass.

She thought about the rose on her vanity.

The one with thorns.

She thought about the way Dylan betrayed every girl he was with.

She thought about the look in Valery's eyes when she talked about survival: sharp, bitter, knowing.

And she thought about Rob.

How his silence wasn't empty, but full of things he couldn't say.

She didn't want to die in this world.

Not like this.

Not as someone else's pretty corpse.

By the time she walked back into the club, it was late.

The lights were dim. Music low. Only a few customers left: men with glazed eyes and fat wallets, looking for distraction. The air was thick with old perfume and sweat.

Rob looked up from the bar.

His face didn't change, but his eyes followed her.

She walked straight past the dressing room.

Straight onto the stage.

No music.

No spotlight.
Just her and the pole and the ghosts in her chest.
She climbed, slow and silent, and wrapped herself
around it like a question she hadn't answered yet.
And then she let go.
Just enough to fall.
Just enough to feel the wind on her skin again.
Just enough to remember that she was still alive.

Chapter 12: The Burn Behind the Eyes

The lights had turned mean.

What used to be glitter now felt like ash. The stage
spun under Starr's heels like a cruel joke, and even
the money stacked, tucked, and thrown, seemed to
mock her. The air inside the club had thickened,
scented with desperation, sweat, and the ghost of
something rotting beneath the surface.
She was back on the white. Hard. She told herself
it was just to get through the nights, just to feel
awake, just to feel something. But the powder
wasn't keeping her up anymore, it was holding her
under, suffocating and sharp. Her heartbeat had
become a metronome for anxiety. Every night was
a high-speed tunnel, and every morning came with
the crash.
Valery noticed, but not with kindness. The once-
golden girl was spiraling herself, and there wasn't
room for compassion. Just jealousy, competition,
and whispered cruelty.
It started with a glance in the mirror, a glance that
turned too long. Valery watching her smear
concealer over a bruise on her jaw.
"Not from dancing, I hope," Valery murmured, her
voice slick with insinuation.

Starr didn't answer. She didn't flinch either. But
the silence cracked something open.

"You're not special anymore," Valery said.
"You're just another one of us now."
Later that night, Starr found her in the locker room, crying in the dark, her hair a tangled halo, mascara bleeding down her cheeks. She was shaking. Her hands kept reaching for her purse like she was looking for something she'd already taken.
"You good?" Starr asked flatly.
"Fuck off," Valery snapped, trying to stand and falling back against the lockers with a loud metallic clang.
"You look like shit."
Valery laughed through her tears, a sharp, broken sound. "And you look like you still think you're better than everyone. Just wait."
"What's that supposed to mean?"
"It means you'll be here next year, same spot, same bruise. Except nobody will remember your name."
Their eyes locked. For a second, Starr wanted to reach out. But something in her clenched instead. Maybe it was pride. Maybe it was fear. Maybe it was the realization that the only thing more terrifying than being alone was seeing someone else survive exactly what you were going through and realizing they were losing.

"I'm not you," Starr whispered.

Valery stood, too fast, eyes wild. "That's what we all say. Until the mirror stops lying."

The dressing room had become a second skin: its smell, its noise, its ghosts. Starr had memorized every creak in the makeup counter, every clatter of heels on the tiles. The scent of sweat and perfume. The muffled sobs behind lockers. The nervous laughs.
But lately, it was quiet. No one talked to her anymore, not even to whisper shit behind her back. She'd burned through too many bridges, skipped too many conversations, floated too far from the center.
So, she focused on the only thing that gave her a taste of control: cocaine.
She wasn't just snorting it now - she was slinging it. A few grams here, a few grams there. To the stockbrokers and burned-out hedge funders who liked their girls high and their secrets hidden. The way they stared at her when she leaned in, the way their eyes lit up when she said, "I got something better than your guy", it gave her a sense of leverage. Power. Delusion.
But the illusion cracked on a Friday night.

He was a regular - Dr. Charles, a plastic surgeon from the Upper East Side. Forty-something, married, reeked of Versace cologne and self-importance. He tipped well, wanted nothing more than conversation and a line of coke to keep his evenings buzzing.

That night, Starr was out. Her dealer had flaked. The city felt dry. Her own stash was down to residue, and she hadn't made enough to cover a refill. Still, she needed his cash.

She found him in the champagne lounge and perched on the velvet banquette beside him.

"You want a hit?" she purred, brushing her fingers against his thigh.

He grinned. "You know me too well."

She left for the dressing room, heart pounding, and tore through her locker. Nothing. Just a crushed packet of mint candies and some Advil. Her eyes landed on the green and white dust collecting at the bottom of her purse.

It looks the same, she told herself. He's drunk. He won't know the difference.

She crushed the mints into a fine powder, added a sprinkle of baby powder to mimic texture, and folded it into a small piece of foil. Her hands shook as she returned to the lounge.

He laid it out on the glass table, rolling a twenty with surgeon precision.

One line. Then another.

His eyes widened, but not with euphoria. He coughed. Again. He blinked and sniffed hard, nostrils flaring.

"This is...this tastes weird," he muttered.

"It's fresh," she said quickly. "Just different. Colombian."

He nodded but didn't look convinced.

Later that week, she found out from Melody that Dr. Charles had been admitted to a private clinic with a severe nasal infection. Something about menthol burns in his sinus tissue. His wife found out. He stopped coming to the club.

And the word started to spread.

Not fast, not loud - but enough.

By the next weekend, fewer of the regulars were asking Starr if she partied. Some looked at her like she was radioactive.

She knew she had to hustle harder.

That's when she pushed it with Nico.

She spotted him by the bar, sweat beading at his brow, shirt half unbuttoned, sipping tequila like it was water. His pupils were blown wide, jaw twitching with need. He was perfect: desperate, careless, hungry.

She slinked up to him like a shadow and whispered, "I've got what you need."

He smiled, nodded, didn't ask questions.

She reached into her boot; the tiny packet already prepped. A quick handoff - easy. Routine.

And then Rob was there.

He didn't scream. Didn't grab. Just stared flat, cold, disappointed.

"Office. Now."

The office was always too clean. It made the mess of her life feel even louder.

She sat, small in the chair, still clutching the empty packet in her sweaty fist.

Rob leaned against the desk; jaw clenched.

"Dealing now?" he asked.

She didn't answer.

"I've seen it all, Charlotte. I've watched girls crash and burn in here. You think you're special?"

She shook her head, eyes down.

"You're not. You're high all the time. You're unreliable. You're reckless. And now you're risking my license, my business, your life."

"I needed the money," she whispered.

"Bullshit," he snapped. "You needed the escape. And now you're selling bad product to people who trust you? Word's going around. Dr. Charles? Really?"

Her throat tightened. "That wasn't... I didn't mean for that to happen."

"You faked coke with mints."

Her eyes burned. "I was desperate."

He stared at her for a long time. And when he spoke again, his voice was quieter, but harder. "This is your last warning. Sell again and you're out. No talk. No drama. Just gone."

She nodded, numb.

"Give me whatever's left."

She handed it over: two more bags tucked in her bra. He tossed them in the trash like they were nothing.

Then he opened the door.

"Go home, Starr. Don't come back until you're sober enough to remember your own name."

She walked out, head down, heart racing, not sure if she'd just been fired or saved.

The dressing room felt like a coffin. The heavy air pressed down on Starr's chest, each breath shallow and desperate. The world had narrowed to the pounding in her skull, the unbearable thrum of her heart, the darkness curling at the edges of her vision.

She couldn't think. Couldn't move. Couldn't even cry properly. The numbness was complete, a void that swallowed her whole.

Her knees hit the floor, and she crumpled there, skin cold despite the sweat pouring down her face. Her fingers clawed at the synthetic carpet, desperate for something real, something to hold onto. But all she found was dust and the bitter taste of failure.

The voices from the club seemed to fade into the background, replaced by a growing roar inside her head. A chaotic storm of memories, flashes of the past she'd buried beneath layers of drugs and dance moves.

Her brother's face, twisted in anger. The nights when she hid in her closet, praying for the silence to last. The way his touch had shattered her, leaving cracks she'd tried to glue shut with everything she had.

Tears burned her eyes but wouldn't fall. She was trapped inside her own body, a ghost drowning in poison.

Then, footsteps, soft but urgent, cut through the haze.

"Starr?" The voice was gentle but filled with alarm.

Aliana appeared, eyes wide, heart breaking at the sight. Her own hands trembled as she knelt beside her friend.

"Hey, hey, I'm here," she murmured, voice steady despite the fear. "You're going to be okay. Just hold on."

Aliana's fingers searched for Starr's wrist, finding the rapid pulse pounding against her skin. She reached into her purse and pulled out a small bottle of water, pressing it to Starr's lips.

"Come on, baby," she urged softly. "Just a little sip."

Starr's mouth opened, a dry rasp, and she swallowed with difficulty. The water was cold, sharp against her burning throat.

Aliana wrapped her arms around her, steadying her like she was made of glass.

"I've got you," she repeated, rocking her gently. "Breathe for me. In… and out."

The darkness tugged at Starr's mind, whispering to let go, to sink deeper into oblivion.

But Aliana's voice anchored her, pulling her back from the edge.

Minutes stretched like hours as Aliana held her, refusing to let her slip away.

When the paramedics arrived, Aliana was still cradling Starr's trembling body, whispering promises she wasn't sure she believed.

As the ambulance doors slammed shut, the dream she'd built, the glamorous nights, the fast money, the dizzying highs cracked open. Through the jagged shards, the life she'd buried bled through, raw and aching.

Starr wasn't just a dancer. She was a survivor. A broken girl clawing for light in a world that kept dragging her into shadows.

———

The sterile white walls of the hospital room were a stark contrast to the dim haze of the club's dressing room. The hum of machines filled the silence, punctuated only by the soft beep of the heart monitor.

Charlotte lay on the narrow bed, pale and fragile, a thin blanket draped over her. The bruises on her arms peeked through the loose hospital gown, silent witnesses to battles no one else saw. Her eyes, glassy but clear, flicked toward the chair by the window where Aliana sat, exhausted but vigilant.

Aliana reached over, gently brushing a stray lock of hair from Charlotte's forehead. "You gave me quite a scare."

Charlotte managed a weak smile. "I'm sorry."

"No apologies," Aliana said softly. "You're here. That's what matters."

They sat in silence for a moment, the weight of unspoken things hanging between them.

Finally, Charlotte broke the quiet. "How did you know? That night, I mean."

Aliana's gaze darkened, her fingers tightening around her own knees. "I've been there. Not exactly the same, but close enough. Pain that no one should carry. The kind that makes you want to disappear."

Charlotte's breath hitched. "You... you know?"

Aliana nodded slowly. "My father. I thought I'd never get out. The shame, the fear - t's a poison. Took me years to fight it off."

Tears welled in Charlotte's eyes, the dam threatening to break. "I thought I was alone."

"You're not," Aliana whispered. "You don't have to be."

Charlotte's voice trembled. "Sometimes, I think about those nights. The silence after. How no one believed me. How I blamed myself."

Aliana's hand found Charlotte's, fingers intertwining. "That's what they want you to think. But you're not the one who broke. You survived."

For the first time in a long while, Charlotte felt a crack in her armor - a fragile hope.

"I'm scared," she admitted. "Scared I'll never be okay."

Aliana smiled, bittersweet but fierce. "Okay doesn't come easy. But it comes. One day at a time."

They sat there, two broken women stitched together by pain and resilience, the beginning of something real.

The second night in the hospital was quieter. Charlotte hadn't slept much, her mind haunted by dreams that felt more like memories: half-real, half-constructed by years of repression. She would wake in the dark, heart racing, certain she'd heard his voice again. But it was just the IV drip. Or the air conditioner clicking on. Or silence.

Aliana stayed curled in the armchair, her hoodie pulled over her knees, still in the same jeans from two nights ago. She hadn't left, not once, not even to go outside. She nursed Charlotte through the fever, helped her use the bathroom, brushed her hair when her arms were too weak to lift. It was the kind of care no one ever gave girls like them. Not without a price.

It was sacred.

Late that night, as the sky outside turned a deep indigo, the hospital door creaked open quietly.

Charlotte turned her head, expecting another nurse. But it wasn't.

It was Lilly.

She looked different.

Her long curls were brushed and shining, her face carefully made up, but her eyes were rimmed in shadows. She wore a sleek black coat that didn't belong to a girl who just came off the subway. There was a different energy to her now - sharper, closed-off, but still very much Lilly underneath.

Charlotte froze.

Aliana stirred awake, narrowing her eyes. She didn't move from her chair, but her posture shifted subtly, protectively.

Lilly stood just inside the doorway, hesitating. Her gaze dropped to Charlotte's arms, the IV, the bruises. Her lips parted, but no words came.

Charlotte broke the silence first. "You came."

"I didn't know what to say," Lilly said softly. "I still don't."

Aliana stood slowly. "Maybe I'll give you two a minute."

She walked past Lilly, brushing her shoulder lightly - not cruel, but not warm either - and disappeared down the hall.

Lilly approached the bed, slow and hesitant. "You look like shit."

Charlotte smiled faintly. "Thanks."

"I mean… you scared me."

Charlotte blinked. "I scared you? You vanished, Lilly."

"I know. I fucked up. I was.." Lilly exhaled hard, sitting down on the edge of the bed. "I was trying to protect myself."

"From me?"

"No. From everything. From that place. From becoming what we swore we wouldn't."

Charlotte looked away. "Too late."

Lilly reached out, her fingers ghosting over Charlotte's hand. "It's not too late. You're still here."

Charlotte let the contact sit for a moment, then looked her in the eyes. "Why'd you really leave?"

Lilly didn't answer right away. When she did, her voice was quieter than it had ever been. "Because I saw what was happening to you. And I saw what was happening to me. And I didn't know how to save either of us."

Charlotte's throat tightened.

"I thought you hated me," she whispered.

"I hated that I couldn't help," Lilly replied. "And I hated that I didn't try."

They sat in silence, breathing in the stale air, full of things left unsaid.

Then Charlotte said something she hadn't said in years, something that had lived under her tongue like a blade.

"My brother used to hurt me."

Lilly didn't flinch.

"He did things," Charlotte continued. "Things I told myself were my fault. And the first time a man touched me in the VIP room, I wasn't even in my body. I was thirteen again."

Tears slipped down Lilly's face, silent and slow. "I didn't know," she said.

"No one did," Charlotte murmured. "And I thought if I made enough money, wore the right heels, had the right man want me... maybe I wouldn't be that girl anymore."

"You're not," Lilly said fiercely. "You're not her. You're more."

Charlotte looked at her, really looked, and saw not just her friend, but someone who'd been fighting her own silent war.

"Stay?" Charlotte asked. "At least for a little."

Lilly nodded, wiping her tears. "I'll stay."

And she did.

She crawled into the hospital bed beside Charlotte, careful not to tug the IV. The two of them lay side by side like they had so many nights in their early twenties, after long shifts, when dreams were still alive and nothing had broken them yet.

In the quiet dark, their fingers found each other's and laced together.

And for the first time in months, Charlotte slept.

Chapter 13: Temptation

The days blurred.

Aliana stayed until her shift at the club resumed, and even then, she sent texts every few hours, checking in, sending photos of their old dressing room with captions like "Not the same without you."
But it was Lilly who never left.
She slept curled on the couch or right beside Charlotte, depending on how bad the shaking got. She held Charlotte's hair back when she vomited. She changed the sheets when the sweating wouldn't stop. She sat through the 3 a.m. cravings, when Charlotte wept and begged to be taken back to the club or just given a bump to stop the ache in her bones.
"It's not just the coke," Charlotte sobbed one night. "It's the way it made me feel. Like I was someone else."
"I know," Lilly said. "But that feeling comes at a price we can't keep paying."
Charlotte's nose bled for two days straight. Her arms trembled uncontrollably. The inside of her mouth was cut from clenching her teeth in her sleep.
And then, slowly, it passed.
The fog began to lift.

By the fifth day, she was able to sit up without collapsing.

On the seventh, she ate solid food.

On the ninth, she showered. By herself. Standing upright.

It felt like a miracle.

But miracles in her world always came with fine print.

Dylan never showed up. Not even a phone call.

This was over long before it even had a slight chance to begin...

That night, after Charlotte had changed into a borrowed hoodie and sat curled in a blanket watching the rain tap the window, Lilly sat down beside her and said the thing that changed everything.

"I want to show you something," she said, pulling her phone from her bag. "No judgment, okay?"

Charlotte nodded.

Lilly swiped through a few messages, then turned the screen toward her.

There was a photo of Lilly in a velvet gown, standing next to a man in a tuxedo. He looked twice her age and ten times her wealth.

"We were in Venice. That was a yacht party. See that necklace? Real sapphires."

Charlotte frowned. "You dating him?"

Lilly exhaled, long and careful. "Not really. Not like that."

Charlotte blinked. "Then what?"

"I'm working for an agency," Lilly said. "High-end escorting. Not like Craigslist bullshit. These are billionaires. Old money. Private jets. The works."

Charlotte stared.

Lilly kept going. "He paid ten thousand for one weekend. All I had to do was smile, wear what he liked, be sweet in public. And yes, sleep with him. But it's safe. Controlled. I make the rules."

Charlotte didn't say anything for a long time.

Then she asked, "And you want me to do it?"

Lilly didn't flinch. "I want you to have options. I know what it's like, when your body feels like the only currency you've got left. But this way... we write the terms."

Charlotte laughed softly, bitter. "Do we?"

Lilly grabbed her hand. "Listen. I've got a trip to London. Gala for some tech investor - old client. He asked if I could bring a friend. Blonde, pretty, American. You'd only need to look good and be charming. No pressure to do anything else. If you say yes, we fly out in three days."

Charlotte stared at the rain.

Something inside her, quiet and bruised, began to stir.

A new world. A new costume. A new stage.

No more sticky poles, grabby hands in back rooms, or trying to convince surgeons and coke dealers to buy another hour of her company. No more standing barefoot in a club bathroom brushing blood off her nostrils.

This was something different.
Or at least, it looked different.
"I don't know," she whispered.
"You don't have to decide now," Lilly said gently. "But just think about it. London, five stars, no strings. A fresh start."
Charlotte looked down at her bruised knuckles, then up at her reflection in the dark glass. She barely recognized herself. But the girl staring back looked like she was ready to shed her skin.
"Okay," she said. "I'll come."
Lilly smiled, wide and sparkling. "Good. You'll need a passport."
"I have one."
Lilly grinned. "Of course you do."
Charlotte didn't sleep much that night.
But when she did, she dreamed of diamonds, chandeliers, and champagne flutes.
She dreamed of being someone else.

The jet touched down in London at dawn.
A sheet of mist hung low over the runway, softening the sharp edges of Heathrow's steel and glass, turning everything to shadow and suggestion. Charlotte leaned her forehead against the tiny oval window, heart pounding with the electric static of insomnia and adrenaline. She

hadn't slept on the flight, not really. Too many champagne flutes. Too much turbulence inside her chest.

Lilly sat beside her in silk and highlighter, already transformed into someone else. Her eyes were rimmed with gold, her lashes impossibly thick. She looked like a Vogue ad Charlotte once tore from a magazine when she used to dream of a different life.

Now she was inside that dream, and it was swallowing her.

They were met at the gate by a driver in a black suit who held a small sign that simply read: "Miss Lily & Guest." He didn't ask their names. He didn't even glance twice at their jet-lagged faces or the way Charlotte clutched her oversized tote like a lifeline.

The car was a Rolls-Royce, the inside stitched with cream leather and silence. As they rolled through the gray dawn streets of London, Charlotte stared at the rows of brick townhouses and Georgian mansions, trying to remember the last time she felt grounded anywhere. Every building looked like it held secrets. Every corner promised something decadent or dangerous.

The hotel was in Mayfair - historic, velvet-draped, so polished it barely seemed real. Staff with clipped accents and discreet eyes opened doors and offered herbal tea. Their suite overlooked a private garden, the trees dripping with morning rain. A crystal chandelier shimmered above a four-poster bed the size of Charlotte's old apartment.

"Welcome to the stage," Lilly said, spinning slowly in the center of the room. "Act One begins now."

Charlotte didn't answer.

She felt it already that tug between awe and nausea. Like watching the world from the edge of a high cliff, swaying on her heels, unsure if she was flying or falling.

Later, after naps and long baths and room service eggs, Lilly handed Charlotte a dress. It was midnight blue, slit to the thigh, backless, sleek as a second skin.

"Try it on," she said. "He'll love that color."

"Who's he?"

"Arthur," Lilly said casually. "Forty-four. Built like a politician. Smiles like he's buying you. Old client. Always generous. Always discreet."

Charlotte pulled the dress on, ignoring the scream of panic in her chest.

"What does he want?" she asked softly.

"Someone beautiful to stand beside him at the gala. Someone to keep him entertained. Someone who listens, laughs at the right moments. And maybe, if the vibe's right, someone who stays the night."

Charlotte stared at herself in the mirror.

The girl in the reflection was a goddess. A vision. But her eyes were storm-dark and tired. She looked like she was playing a role she hadn't rehearsed enough to survive.

"Can I say no?" Charlotte asked.

"Always," Lilly said. "But if you do, just know, someone else will say yes."

The line hit like a slap.

Charlotte turned away from the mirror. "Fine. Let's go play dress-up."

The gala was held at a grand 18th-century mansion where the aristocracy once toasted to empires and buried their scandals in velvet salons.

Charlotte stepped from the car into a dreamscape of camera flashes and murmured greetings. The red carpet gleamed beneath her stilettos. A hedge of paparazzi pressed against gold stanchions, flashes blinking like the eyes of curious beasts.

No one knew her name.

But everyone looked.

She walked beside Lilly like a ghost draped in satin, her bare back kissed by the cold London air, every inch of her body rehearsed in elegance. It wasn't the club. This was quieter, crueler. Here, power wore silk gloves and thousand-dollar cologne. Here, eyes cut like glass.

Inside, the mansion glowed.

Chandeliers like galaxies. Champagne pyramids.
Live strings playing a sultry cover of "Sweet
Dreams (Are Made of This)." Waiters in tuxedos
moved like shadows. Oil paintings stared from
their golden frames, judging.

Arthur appeared near the entrance staircase—gray
temples, sculpted jaw, dressed in a Tom Ford
tuxedo that likely cost more than Charlotte made
in a month at the club. He smiled like he knew
everything.

"Lilly," he said warmly, kissing her cheek.
"You've outdone yourself."

Then his eyes landed on Charlotte.

And lingered.

"This must be your friend," he said, offering his
hand. "Charming."

"Charlotte," she said, shaking it.

His palm was soft, his touch- brief. But she felt the
transaction click into place, like a credit card
processing. His gaze trailed along her collarbone,
dipped down her dress, then rose again with a
practiced smile.

"You'll be perfect," he said.

She wasn't sure what he meant.

They floated into the crowd: art dealers,
ambassadors, tech moguls, royal cousins.

Everyone gleamed. Everyone knew someone.

Charlotte sipped champagne and smiled like her
life depended on it. Because maybe it did.

Arthur kept a loose hand on her back.

He introduced her as "a friend from New York," which felt like both a compliment and a leash. She played the part: laughed at his stories, nodded when his colleagues talked about real estate and climate investments, accepted compliments with an airy shrug.

But the whole time, her mind swam.

She was high on elegance and low-grade panic. Every time Arthur leaned in close to whisper a joke, she smelled the $400 scotch on his breath and wondered how many girls had stood in this exact spot. Every time he touched her back, the hairs on her neck rose like they were trying to escape.

She caught Lilly's eye across the room.

Lilly winked. Lifted her glass.

Charlotte lifted hers too.

The game was simple. Be beautiful. Be charming. Don't let anyone see the girl who once sobbed in a club locker room with blood on her heels.

Later, as the crowd thinned and the music softened, Arthur led her out to a terrace overlooking the park.

"You've done well tonight," he said. "Natural grace. Most girls try too hard."

Charlotte smiled faintly. "I used to be on stage. Old habits."

He turned toward her; eyes heavy-lidded now.
"And what are you now?
She hesitated. "Still figuring that out."
Arthur studied her. "You're a chameleon. That's good. In my world, adaptability is everything."
A beat of silence.
"Would you like to join me for a nightcap?" he asked. "Nothing expected. Just a little more conversation."
Charlotte looked out at the park. A double-decker bus rolled past like a memory from a film.
She thought of her mother.
She thought of her brother.
She thought of the crushed mint candy and the doctor's bleeding nose.
Then she looked back at Arthur.
And smiled.
"Sure," she said. "One drink."
Arthur's penthouse suite sat above a big green park, encased in glass and stillness. No noise reached them there, just the hum of the city far below, like a ghost breathing through the floorboards.
The butler disappeared after pouring a single malt into two crystal tumblers. Charlotte stood at the window, watching headlights flicker through the trees like fireflies lost in fog. Her reflection hovered over the night skyline: bare shoulders, lips stained plum, eyes that didn't blink.

Arthur moved with the ease of someone used to owning space. His jacket came off. His shoes were already gone. He loosened his tie and handed her a drink without asking how she took it.

"To old souls in young bodies," he said.

She raised her glass. The scotch bit the back of her throat. She swallowed too fast, pretending it didn't hurt.

Arthur sat beside her on the velvet couch, not touching her yet, but close. "You remind me of someone," he said after a while.

"Who?"

"My daughter's piano teacher," he said with a low laugh. "But sexier. More damaged."

Charlotte froze.

She tried to laugh, but it came out like a cough.

"That's… an interesting compliment."

He leaned back, unfazed. "It's not meant to offend. Most men are afraid to admit they're drawn to ruin. But it's true. We see a crack in something beautiful and we want to press our fingers inside."

She drained her drink. Her body buzzed, but her nerves stayed raw.

Arthur reached for her hand. His palm was cool. Heavy.

"You're trembling," he said.

"I'm tired."

"You don't have to stay, you know," he murmured. "You can go. I won't chase."

Charlotte looked at him. For a second, one long breath, it seemed possible. That she could slip out, take the elevator down, vanish into the fog and forget this ever happened.

But then he added, "But if you stay, I'll take care of you. Not just tonight. I'm generous. I remember good company."

Something in her chest twisted.

This wasn't strip-club sleaze. This wasn't money rained down from drunk stockbrokers or frat boys demanding love they couldn't name. This was colder. Cleaner. More calculated.

He didn't want her body. He wanted her silence.

She reached for the second glass.

They didn't speak for a while. Outside, the rain started again. A faint drumbeat on the windows. She sat close enough to him to feel the heat of his thigh. Close enough to know this was the point of no return.

"Tell me something true," Arthur said suddenly.

"What?"

"Anything. One real thing."

Charlotte thought of her brother. Of the old barn. Of her knees in the dirt and the sound of summer insects screaming while he zipped up his jeans.

She opened her mouth.

And said instead, "I used to think I'd be a writer. I used to make up poems on receipts. I had a drawer full of them back home."

Arthur smiled. "That's lovely. Poets are dangerous. They feel everything too much."
He leaned in.
His lips brushed hers - light, calculated. She didn't pull away.
But inside, her skin screamed.
It wasn't that he was cruel. Or ugly. Or even wrong.
It was that he saw her as a blank page.
And she wasn't.
She was a burned diary.
Still, when he led her to the bedroom, she didn't resist. She undressed like it was a ritual: silent, numb. She lay beneath him and stared at the crown molding, thinking of constellations she could name. She let him kiss her throat and stroke her ribs. He whispered something about how fragile she felt, like glass, like crystal.
After, she showered with the water too hot, until her skin flushed raw.
Arthur had already dozed off.
In the mirror, steam-coated, Charlotte caught her own eyes.
And hated herself a little less than she expected to.
Because at least this time, it was a choice.
Even if it broke her.

Charlotte woke to sunlight slashing through the penthouse blinds like blades. Arthur was already gone. A folded note sat beside a breakfast tray she hadn't touched eggs congealing, a silver pot of untouched coffee.

Thank you for your company. Let's speak soon. - A.

Even his handwriting was elegant.

Charlotte swung her legs over the edge of the bed and stared at her knees. A faint bruise was blooming on her thigh, she couldn't remember how it got there. Maybe she'd bumped into the marble tub. Maybe she didn't want to remember. She dressed in the same gown from the night before, its sequins like fish scales, still reeking faintly of perfume and Arthur's skin. She didn't bother fixing her hair.

The doorman hailed her a car without a word. He knew what she was. Or thought he did.

By the time she returned to the hotel suite she shared with Lilly, it was noon. London burned grey outside the window, fog-drenched and quiet, like a city mourning something only the two of them could feel.

Lilly was on the couch, barefoot in a silk robe, sipping green tea.

Charlotte stood in the doorway for a long moment before saying anything.

"So," Lilly said softly. "How was your night?"

Charlotte closed the door and leaned against it.
"Fine."
"Just fine?"
She nodded, then shook her head. "I don't know."
Lilly watched her with an unreadable expression.
"You didn't have to do it, you know."
"I did."
"No, you didn't."
Charlotte walked past her and sat on the edge of
the bed. Her hands shook when she reached for the
water bottle.
"I thought I could do it like you do," she
whispered.
"Do what?"
"Detach. Smile. Get through it."
Lilly stood and crossed the room. She sat beside
her and took her hand gently, almost like a mother.
"You think I'm detached?" she asked. "I have to
get drunk to walk into half those rooms. I throw up
after the worst ones. I disassociate so hard
sometimes I forget my own name. Don't you ever
think I enjoy this, babe."
Charlotte looked up, startled by the cracks in
Lilly's mask.
"But why… why keep doing it?"
Lilly's mouth twisted into something like a smile -
sad and bitter. "Because I don't know what else
I'd be good at. Because I like the money. Because
sometimes, I feel powerful, like I'm holding all
their secrets in my hands."

They were silent for a moment.

"Did he hurt you?" Lilly asked softly.

"No. He was polite. Kind, even. But… he looked at me like I was a piece of steak. Not a person."

"That's the job," Lilly said. "They're not paying for your soul. Just the performance."

Charlotte's chest tightened.

"But I felt empty," she said. "Hollow. Like I left myself in New York and sent the shell to London."

Lilly nodded. "You'll get used to it. Or you'll leave."

Charlotte turned to her. "Have you ever been in love?"

Lilly laughed - a real, broken sound. "Once. Back in Chicago. He was a bartender with hands like fire and too many dreams. I told him I danced to pay for college. He found out the truth. Left a note and never came back."

Charlotte felt the ache bloom again - lonely and unspoken. "I don't know if I've ever been in love. I don't think I even know how to trust."

Lilly touched her cheek. "That's not your fault."

And suddenly, Charlotte was crying.

Not the pretty tears she'd perfected at the club. Not the mascara-streaked kind that bought sympathy and tips. These were hot, choking sobs pulled from her gut. She curled into Lilly's lap like a child, like someone she hadn't been since long before the stage name, the glitter, the noise.

Lilly held her. Didn't speak. Just stroked her hair like a sister or something more sacred.

When the sobs faded, Charlotte whispered, "I miss myself."

Lilly kissed her forehead. "We'll find her. You're still in there somewhere."

Charlotte wiped her eyes and sat up. "He wants to see me again."

"Will you?"

"I don't know. I think I need to go to New York first."

They sat like that for a while, London spinning quietly outside, two girls wrapped in silk and grief. Charlotte didn't know what she would say to Arthur. Or to Dylan. Or even to herself. But she knew the mirror had cracked open.

And something honest was starting to beat again.

The plane touched down in New York just after midnight. Rain slicked the runway, and the city glimmered like a bruised jewel in the dark. Charlotte didn't go home.

She went straight to the club.

It was almost muscle memory now - sliding through the velvet curtain, catching the perfume-clouded air, the rhythmic thump of bass that lived in her bones. Her stilettos echoed against the back hallway floor. She passed by the mirror-lined walls where a dozen girls preened, pouted, powdered.

Someone yelled her name.

"Starr!"

Valery. Already drunk. Or worse.

"Back from London like royalty," Valery slurred. "Come kiss me, Queen."

Charlotte gave her a soft smile and slipped past. She didn't want to talk to anyone. Not yet.

She opened her locker and just stared into it. Glitter heels. Perfume. A torn Polaroid from two summers ago. Lipstick that had melted and re-hardened in unnatural shapes. Everything exactly the same, and yet... everything wrong.

When she sat down on the cracked bench, her knees felt too old for her age.

Rob appeared a moment later. Quiet as always.

"You look like you aged a year in a week," he said.

Charlotte smirked. "Feels like it."

"Wanna talk?"

She hesitated. Then nodded.

They walked to his office - low light, a broken fan spinning half-heartedly in the corner. The walls were still covered in old posters and forgotten rules.

Rob poured her a cup of coffee. It tasted like cardboard and memories.

"I saw the security report from last month," he said.

Charlotte blinked. "Which part?"

"The mint incident. And a few other nights you weren't... steady."

She didn't answer.

"I didn't write it up. I could've. Should've. But I didn't."

"Why not?"

"Because I know when a girl's drowning," Rob said. "And I thought maybe... you'd figure out how to swim again."

Charlotte's throat tightened.

"I've been trying to come back up for air," she whispered.

"Did you?"

She thought about London. About the gala. About Arthur's hand on her back. About Lilly's voice in the dark. About the moment she cried on a silk couch and felt something break open.

"Almost," she said.

"Do you want to stay?"

Charlotte looked at him - really looked. His tired eyes. His knowing silence. He wasn't just the manager. He was the lighthouse. And maybe the warning.

"I don't think I can," she said.

He nodded once. "You were one of the best we ever had. But I knew this place would kill your soul if you stayed too long."

A beat passed between them.

"Rob?"

"Yeah?"

"Thank you."

"For what?"

"For seeing me."

He didn't smile. Just touched her shoulder gently.

"You gonna tell Dylan?" he asked.

Charlotte sighed. "I guess I have to."

Dylan found her later that night. In the back hallway near the bar, where the lights were low and the noise couldn't quite reach.

"You look like you've been through war," he said, leaning against the wall with that same boyish grin.

"Maybe I have, and you were not there" she replied.

He studied her, as if trying to measure who she'd become since their last conversation.

"Are you're thinking about quitting."

Charlotte nodded.

He stepped closer. "What if I asked you to stay?"

She tilted her head. "Why?"

"Because I like you. Because I feel something with you I've never felt before."

"That's not enough."

Dylan's face darkened.

"You think I don't see the real you?"

"I think you don't want to," she said. "Because the real me is broken in ways you can't fix."

He reached for her wrist, but she stepped back.

He didn't argue. Not really. Just watched her, lips pressed into a bitter line.

"You'll regret this," he said finally.

"Maybe," she whispered. "But at least the regret will be mine."

She turned and walked away, not toward the stage, not toward the dressing room, but out.

Out the back door.

Into the cold, damp night.

And for the first time in months, Charlotte felt like she could breathe.

Chapter 14: New Skins

Charlotte didn't tell the other girls she was leaving, not even Valery, who probably wouldn't have noticed anyway. She kept the decision folded inside her like a secret letter, one she reread every night in the blue hour before sleep.

The apartment was half-empty now. She'd sold her furniture to a neighbor and left behind a pile of glittering dresses in a garbage bag, along with a broken glass tray, a box of makeup smudged with powder, and a bundle of old Polaroids. The air smelled like finality and something else she couldn't name. She packed her suitcase quietly, folding her lingerie with care, rolling stockings into tight little spirals, placing her heels in their cloth bags. She left the mirror uncovered.
When the car came, the driver helped with her bag and said her name like it belonged to someone else. "Miss Charlotte?"
She nodded and slid into the backseat. Rain had started falling again, that thin New York rain that coated everything with grime. She watched the city drift past her window like a funeral procession: bodegas shuttering for the night, flashing neon signs, a man dragging a cart of aluminum cans through a red light. There was nothing left to take with her. Not even herself.

At JFK, the terminal was bright and sterile. She didn't check a bag. Just her carry-on and a purse full of quiet ghosts. While waiting to board, she stared at her reflection in the airport window. It was thinner now. Harder. There were faint shadows under her eyes and her lips were chapped despite the lipstick. The screen above her blinked with updates: DELAYED, ON TIME, NOW BOARDING. Time moved in strange shapes.

On the plane, she took a window seat and watched raindrops streak the glass like tears that weren't hers. She didn't sleep. She couldn't. Every time she closed her eyes, she saw Lilly's invitation flickering in her mind like a match: Come to London. It's different here. There's more power.

There had been champagne that night, and a dress so expensive she was afraid to touch it. And Arthur, his hands cold, his voice like honey poured over knives.

She had said yes because she wanted to be reborn. She had said yes because she was tired of dying in pieces.

Eight hours passed like a dream without color.

Heathrow was chaos: grey light, sharp British accents, the smell of coffee and cold metal. Charlotte moved through it like a ghost in designer boots. Her coat was long, black, and cinched at the waist. She wore dark sunglasses even though the sun hadn't bothered to show up.

Lilly was waiting just outside customs, a cigarette in one hand and her phone in the other. Her hair was slicked back, lips red, heels high and unapologetic. She looked like someone who belonged on marble, not pavement.
"Darling," she said, flicking ash onto the sidewalk. "You look like you haven't slept in a week. Good. They like them hollow."

Charlotte didn't answer. She let Lilly kiss both cheeks and take her arm like they were old friends at a funeral. A black car idled at the curb, windows tinted, the driver in a cap and gloves. Inside, the car smelled like money. Leather, perfume, and a faint trace of expensive cigars. Lilly poured her a glass of champagne from a silver bottle chilling in a hidden compartment. "To new beginnings," she said, lifting her glass. Charlotte sipped. It tasted like nothing.
London passed by the window: slick buildings, black cabs, red buses, wet stone streets that looked hundreds of years old. It felt cleaner than New York, but colder. Less forgiving. The sky hung low, bruised and damp.

"You're not a girl anymore," Lilly said, swirling her glass. "You're a weapon now. Understand?"

Charlotte nodded. She didn't, not really. But it was the kind of thing Lilly said when she wanted you to believe you were special.

The flat was in Kensington- a two-bedroom, clean lines, sharp corners, minimalist furniture in shades of white and grey. There was a marble kitchen she wouldn't cook in, a soaking tub she wouldn't use, and a view of the city that made her feel small and sharp at the same time.

"This is temporary," Lilly said. "A holding cell until you're out there full-time."

Charlotte touched the glass wall with her fingertips. London looked blurred and unreachable. "What if I'm not ready?" she asked. Lilly laughed, tossing her cigarette pack on the counter. "You were ready the minute you left that club."

That night, they didn't go out. Lilly cooked pasta, barefoot and in silk. They sat on the couch with plates in their laps, wine in tall glasses, and music playing low in the background, something sad and seductive.

"You'll see," Lilly said, barefoot knees curled beneath her. "These men aren't like the ones at the club. They're cultured. Rich. Discreet. They don't want a showgirl. They want an experience. That's why they'll pay ten grand a night."

Charlotte stared into her wine. "And what do I want?"

Lilly smiled like someone who'd forgotten how. "You'll figure that out when it's too late."

They sat in silence after that.

Outside, the city lights bled into the mist. Charlotte felt it all press against the glass, the past, the promise, the thousand versions of herself that had died already.

His name was Sebastian.

Lilly didn't give her a photo, just a name, a hotel, and a script.

"He's old money. Family estate in the countryside. He likes conversation. Intelligence. Red wine. Silk."

Charlotte had nodded like it was a business meeting. In a way, it was. But it felt different than dancing, it felt less frantic, more precise. Here, the mask didn't slip because it had been stitched on from the moment she said yes.

The hotel was somewhere near Mayfair. Elegant in that stiff British way, brass and velvet, slow elevators, fireplaces that weren't just for show. Charlotte wore black again. A silk gown with a thigh slit. No bra. Her perfume was faint, floral, haunting. She knocked on the suite door once and waited.

Sebastian was older than Arthur. Late fifties, maybe early sixties. Tall, trim, the kind of face that had once been striking and now simply looked expensive. He greeted her with a glass of wine and a kiss on the cheek.

"You're American," he said, amused. "I do like the accent."

"You'll like more than that," she said, surprised at the smoothness of her voice. Like she had swallowed someone far more composed.

They sat in velvet armchairs and talked about art. He showed her a rare book he kept on the side table. He spoke of a ruined abbey in Wales where he sometimes went to think. He touched her knee only once during dinner.

There was no rush.

When he finally led her into the bedroom, he asked her to undress slowly. She did it like ritual, one strap, then the other, gown sliding to the floor like a whispered secret. She didn't tremble, not even when he touched her jaw and whispered, "You're quite the illusion."

Quick. Steady. Overwhelming.

Afterward, he lay beside her and asked about her life. She gave him half-truths, carefully dressed: a dancer, a hostess, not looking for love but something quieter. He traced circles on her back and said, "You seem like you've been broken more than once."

"I have," she replied.

Sebastian didn't ask for details.

In the morning, he was gone. A thick envelope sat on the side table beneath a single tulip in a crystal vase. Red. The same color as the lipstick she left on the wine glass.

Charlotte showered, dressed, and slipped back into the street like it had never happened. But something had. She didn't know what yet.

She walked through London with bare hands and a burning throat, the envelope heavy in her coat pocket. The money didn't feel like guilt. It felt like control. Like currency in a game, she'd finally learned to play.

She called Lilly.

"How was he?" Lilly asked.

"Polite. Clean. Gentle."

"And?"

"I didn't hate it."

"That's how it begins," Lilly said, almost sweetly. "Soon you'll start to forget where the mask ends."

Three days after Sebastian, a package arrived. It was wrapped in black paper with a cream ribbon and no return address. Inside: a small, red box from Cartier. Nestled in velvet was a delicate bracelet: white gold, thin as breath, with a single diamond at its center. There was no note, but she didn't need one.

Arthur.

Charlotte held it between her fingers like it might burn her. She hadn't thought of him much since that night at the gala. She'd tried not to. But now he was back, not as a man, but as a gesture. A gift that weighed more than it should.

Lilly looked up from her espresso when she walked into the kitchen. "He sent something, didn't he?"

Charlotte nodded, setting the box on the counter like a confession.

"Wear it or don't," Lilly said, lighting a cigarette. "But understand that once you accept the gifts, you've entered his orbit."

Charlotte said nothing. She poured herself coffee, black and bitter. She hadn't decided whether she was staying or leaving. She hadn't decided anything. But she felt it - the gravity of Arthur's world, subtle and silent, pulling her in.

Later that afternoon, she sat alone on the couch, bracelet in hand. It was beautiful. Impossibly delicate. The kind of thing a girl like her was never supposed to own unless it was bought - unless it came at a price.

She thought of her mother's wrist, thick and work worn. Of her father's absence. Of her brother's breath in her ear when she was too small to understand what was being taken.

And then she slipped it on.

It was cold at first, like a lie. But it fit perfectly. That night, she dreamt of the club again. The velvet couches, the sticky lights, the faces in the dark. She saw Dylan, blurred and unreachable. She saw Rob, arms crossed, disappointment in his eyes. And she saw herself in the mirror, bruised and nose-bleeding, trying to wipe away something that had already seeped into her bones.

She woke up sweating.

Lilly was in the kitchen, making tea in an oversized sweater. She didn't ask what Charlotte had dreamt. She just poured two mugs and handed one over, her eyes rimmed with old kohl and new exhaustion.

"Arthur wants to see you again," she said.

Charlotte looked down at the bracelet.

"I figured," she whispered.

The car came at dusk.

Not a limo this time, but a sleek black town car with privacy glass and the smell of soft leather inside. Charlotte wore red. Not club red, no fishnets or fake lashes, but a gown Lilly had loaned her, clingy and understated. Her makeup was light. Her hair pinned. A single spray of perfume at her collarbone.

Arthur opened the door of his Chelsea townhouse himself. He looked older in his own space - less polished, more human. No butler. No staff. Just a man in a navy cashmere sweater who smiled as if they'd known each other for years.

"You wore it," he said, nodding to the bracelet.

She did not smile. "Yes."

Dinner was Coq au vin, roasted vegetables, and a wine she couldn't pronounce. Charlotte didn't ask the year or the vineyard. She let him pour it, her fingers trembling slightly around the glass.

Arthur watched her the entire time, not leering but assessing. Like she was a piece of art he hadn't decided how to hang.

"Why did you send the bracelet?" she asked.

"Because I thought of you," he said plainly.

Charlotte leaned forward. "Was it guilt? Gratitude?"

Arthur chuckled. "Does it matter?"

"It does to me."

He set his wine down. "You remind me of someone," he said. "Someone I knew when I was young."

Charlotte tilted her head. "A lover?"

Arthur smiled faintly. "No. A ghost."

She waited.

He turned toward her, eyes a little glazed.

"I've got three months left, Charlotte. Maybe less."

Her lips parted.

"I have heart failure," he continued. "Not the fixable kind. It's genetic. Came on slow. Quietly. But I'm at the end now."

She didn't know what to say. "I'm… I'm sorry."

He nodded.

"I've done everything right. Ate the vegetables. Hired the best doctors. Paid for the best stem cell treatments. Still…" he gestured at his chest, almost amused. "It just… gave out. Isn't that something?"

Charlotte searched his face, looking for signs of illness, of weakness, of the man behind the mask. She saw sadness. And maybe fear.

"I don't want to die," he said softly. "Not yet. Not when I've spent my whole life building everything."

Charlotte placed her hand over his, gentle.

He looked at her for a long moment. "You're very kind."

Then he said something that made her stomach clench:

"Wouldn't it be beautiful, to leave this world carrying a piece of someone like you?"

She blinked. "What?"

Arthur smiled faintly. "Sorry. Morbid thought."

Charlotte stared at her plate, her appetite gone.

This time, when they went upstairs, she didn't feel like a girl slipping into someone else's story. She knew where her shoes were. She knew where the exits were. And she knew what this was.

Arthur undressed slowly, as if he wanted to be seen. His body was aging but strong. His hands were warm. He kissed her neck with careful reverence, and when he whispered her name, it was like a hymn. Not to her. To the idea of her.

She didn't feel loved. But she felt powerful.

Afterward, he asked her nothing. He simply placed another envelope on the dresser and kissed her palm.

When she left the townhouse, the cold slapped her face. She didn't call Lilly. She didn't call anyone. She walked the long way back to the flat, her heels echoing against the damp London pavement.

Halfway there, she ducked into a public bathroom, locked the stall, and counted the money.
Ten crisp thousand-pound notes. Neat. Heavy.
Her heart pounded, not from shame, but from clarity.
She didn't feel dirty. She didn't feel clean either.

She felt like someone new.
Someone dangerous.

The flat was quiet when Charlotte returned.
Lilly was curled up on the velvet couch in a silk
robe, glass of red wine in hand, flipping through a
fashion magazine she wasn't really reading. She
didn't look up when Charlotte walked in, but the
tension in her spine said everything.
"You went," she said.
Charlotte dropped her coat on the chair. "I did."
Lilly set her glass down and folded the magazine
closed with surgical precision.
"Was it awful?" she asked.
Charlotte sat beside her, took a breath. "No. It
wasn't awful. It wasn't anything I didn't expect."
Lilly looked at her, eyes narrowing. "But?"
Charlotte ran her hands through her hair, still
damp from the shower at Arthur's place. "It felt
like power. For a minute. But then… it felt like
surrender."
Lilly didn't answer immediately. She stood,
crossed to the window, stared out at the glittering
city beyond. "It always does. Until it doesn't."
Charlotte leaned back into the couch, her body
still sore in places she didn't want to think about.
"Do you ever feel like it's using you up, piece by
piece?"
Lilly turned. "Every day. But I choose it."

Charlotte nodded slowly. "I didn't think I would feel so... separate from myself. Like I was watching it happen. Like I was playing someone else."

"You are," Lilly said. "That's the job."

Charlotte's throat tightened. "And when the act ends?"

Lilly looked tired. Not club-tired. Not hangover tired. But tired in her bones. "Then you go home. You eat something. You pour a drink. You stare in the mirror until you can find your face again."

Charlotte's eyes filled before she could stop them. "I thought I could do this."

"You can," Lilly said, crossing the room again. She crouched in front of her, gripping Charlotte's hands. "But you have to know what it is. You're not playing with dolls anymore. These men will buy pieces of you if you let them. Your silence. Your memories. Your shame. You have to decide what you're selling, and what's never on the table."

Charlotte shook her head. "I don't even know the difference yet."

Lilly smiled, soft and sad. "That's okay. You will."

They sat in silence, the air between them full of unspoken history. The city buzzed beyond the window, cold and alive. Charlotte looked at her reflection in the glass - blurred, twin-eyed, unknown.

She'd taken the money. She'd worn the bracelet. She'd kissed the man. And none of it had broken her.

But she could feel the fracture forming.

Charlotte stood at the window long after Lilly had gone to bed.
The glass was cool under her fingertips. London blinked below her like a promise whispered through fog: unreal, unfinished. She should have felt powerful. She should have felt rich.

But her mind wandered.
Back to the club.
Back to the night the mirror cracked.
It had started like any other shift - heels, lashes, powdered cheekbones. Fake lashes like wings she no longer believed in. She remembered the white sparkly dress - long, skin-tight, worn too many nights. The one that used to make her feel like a weapon.
Lines on glass. Whispered names. Cold sweat. She danced for a faceless man with teeth too white and a hand too eager.
He pressed a hundred into her G-string and pulled her close, whispering something that made her skin crawl.
"You're just like her," he said. "My sister."

Her body froze.

The music kept playing, but she couldn't hear it anymore. The lights blurred. The man laughed softly, his hand brushing the back of her neck, just like her brother used to when she was twelve.

That was when she ran.

Out of the VIP room. Into the dressing room. Locking the door. Gasping like the oxygen had been poisoned.

She looked in the mirror.

Mascara streaked. Nose bleeding again. Skin blotchy from the powder and panic. She didn't see Starr. She didn't see Charlotte.

Now, in this quiet flat in London, she pressed her forehead against the glass and whispered, "I'm still her."

She didn't know if that was grief or truth.

She didn't know which was worse.

The message came the next morning.

Lilly was already in the kitchen when Charlotte stumbled out of the guest room. There was fresh coffee, avocado toast, and a silence that felt carefully constructed.

Lilly handed her the phone. "Arthur's friend. Philippe."

Charlotte blinked at the screen. A short message, elegant and clear:

"He said you intrigued him. He's hosting a private weekend in the Riviera. He wants us both there. First-class tickets, villa on the coast, all expenses covered."

Charlotte stared at the words. The characters didn't feel real. It read like a scene from someone else's life.

"He's French?" she asked.

"Richer than Arthur," Lilly said. "And colder. Think yachts, caviar, and men who never apologize."

Charlotte sipped her coffee, feeling the bitterness settle into her bones. "What does he want?"

Lilly tilted her head. "What they always want. A story to tell their friends in whispers. A night to replay. A woman who disappears after."

Charlotte's stomach turned. "Do you trust him?"

Lilly hesitated. "Enough to fly there. Not enough to sleep."

Charlotte looked out the window. It was raining again. The London gray was beautiful in its own mournful way. Like the city had agreed to carry your secrets in silence.

The offer lingered between them like patchouli - sweet, seductive, and a little sickening.

"Why me?" Charlotte asked.

Lilly shrugged. "You look like someone they haven't broken yet."

Charlotte ran a hand through her hair. "And if I say no?"

Lilly's eyes softened. "Then you stay. Or you leave. It's not a trap, Charlotte. It's a choice."

Charlotte exhaled slowly. Her body still ached in invisible places. Her mind buzzed with too many memories: Neil, Victor, the mirror, the dressing room floor.

But somewhere underneath the noise... was a spark. A question.

What if she didn't run anymore?

What if she walked into the fire with her eyes open?

She looked at the phone again. The message hadn't changed. But something inside her had.

"Okay," she said softly. "I'll go."

Lilly smiled, not triumphantly, but with something closer to recognition. "I thought you would."

Charlotte finished her coffee and set the cup down. Her hands were steady.

The game had changed.

And she was ready to play.

Chapter 15 - Two Lives

The car smelled like citrus and leather. A black
Mercedes idled by the curb at the private jet
terminal in Nice, the air thick with sea salt and
afternoon sun. Charlotte stepped out into the
warmth, blinking beneath her oversized
sunglasses, her legs still tingling from the short
flight. The driver opened the door with military
precision, and she slid in beside Lilly, who was
already scrolling through her phone, indifferent to
the decadence.

Charlotte tried not to stare out the window like a
tourist, but everything about the Côte d'Azur was
blinding, too perfect, too clean. Villas dotted the
cliffs like expensive ornaments. Palms swayed
theatrically along the coast. Even the clouds
looked like they'd been placed there on purpose.

"This is Philippe's guy?" Charlotte asked,
lowering her voice.

Lilly didn't look up. "Of course. Just relax. We're
here for a good time, not a contract negotiation."

But Charlotte could feel it already: the pressure,
the unspoken script. This wasn't a trip; it was a
performance. One where forgetting a line could
cost more than applause.

When they arrived at the villa, Charlotte had to
catch her breath. The house was perched on a
cliff's edge, blindingly white, with floor-to-

ceiling windows that opened onto a glittering blue horizon. An infinity pool stretched into the sea. Inside, the floors gleamed. Marble. Everything was cream, glass, gold. A curated silence hummed in the air: no clutter, no scent of real life. A woman with a chignon and discreet pearl earrings handed them chilled towels and flutes of champagne. "Welcome to La Maison Premier," she said in a precise French accent. "Monsieur Philippe will join you for dinner."

Lilly smiled easily, used to this rhythm. Charlotte tried to mirror it, but something inside her had knotted tight. She took the champagne but didn't drink it. Her stomach was already glass.

She unpacked slowly in her room, if it could even be called that. The suite had a terrace that opened onto the sea, a canopy bed draped in sheer linen, and a bathtub big enough to drown in. On the dresser, someone had placed a Cartier box. Inside was a necklace. Emeralds. Not even her color.

She left it closed.

Outside, the world shimmered like a fantasy. Inside, Charlotte felt like an understudy thrown on stage, smiling in silk, unsure if the audience had noticed the crack in her voice.

But the curtain was already rising.

The dining room was made of glass. Or at least it felt that way, clear walls opening onto the darkening Mediterranean, the moon climbing out of the sea like a diamond. A long, modern table was set with white orchids and flickering candles. Philippe was already seated at the head.

He stood when they entered. "Eye candy," he said, kissing Lilly on both cheeks, then pausing before Charlotte with a slower smile. "And the new one."

Charlotte offered her hand. His grip was soft but deliberate, like a man used to handling things that break easily.

He was older than she expected. Late fifties, maybe. Expensive tan. Impeccable watch. The kind of man who had never once packed his own suitcase.

"Charlotte, is it?" he asked, gesturing for her to sit. "Enchanted."

She nodded. "Thank you for having me."

Philippe watched her the way a collector watches an auction piece: evaluating the curve, the silence, the effort. "You're American?"

"Yes."

"Beautiful and exotic," he said, turning to Lilly with amusement. "You always bring me such interesting gifts."

Charlotte wanted to hate that word "gift", but she smiled anyway. Her lips moved before her heart could protest.

The food arrived in delicate portions, plated like sculpture. Truffle risotto. Lobster tail. Something foamed and meaningless. Charlotte barely touched hers. The conversation was light: travel, art, some billionaire's yacht that Philippe was considering buying. But there was an undercurrent beneath it, a private theater only the three of them understood.

By the second glass of wine, Philippe was more animated. "Tell me, Charlotte, what do you do when you're not being stunning?"

Lilly jumped in. "She's new to this world. Just finding her footing."

Philippe's gaze didn't move. "I asked her."

Charlotte took a breath. "I used to dance. In New York."

"Ah, a ballerina?"

Lilly laughed. "Not quite."

Charlotte's throat tightened. "Something like that."

Philippe seemed pleased. "So, you already know how to perform."

It wasn't a question.

The staff moved like ghosts, replacing plates, refreshing glasses. Outside, the wind picked up. Charlotte could hear the sea crashing somewhere below. She realized then: the house had no sound except the curated noise of opulence. No TV. No music. No chaos.

Just money and its expectations.

After dessert - an impossible arrangement of figs and lavender, Philippe stood. "Shall we have a nightcap by the fire?"

Charlotte's body tensed. Lilly placed a hand on her wrist beneath the table. Gentle pressure. A warning. A comfort. Both.

In the lounge, Philippe poured brandy into crystal tumblers. Charlotte took a sip, the heat sliding down her throat like regret. She perched on the velvet settee while he stood by the fireplace, talking about markets and power and Monaco's secrets.

Lilly excused herself first, just after midnight. She looked tired, though her makeup was still perfect, a smudge of silver shadow catching the light as she leaned in to kiss Charlotte's cheek. "You'll be fine," she whispered.

Warm breath. Soft lips. A lie disguised as comfort.

Then she slipped into the back seat of the waiting limo, smiling politely to the driver, her heels clicking against the pavement like nothing was wrong.

Then it was just them.

Philippe crossed the room slowly and sat beside her. "You're different," he said, setting his glass down. "Not like the others."

Charlotte tried to laugh. "Isn't that what everyone always says?"

"No. Not always." He leaned in. "There's a sadness in you. Something raw. I find that… intoxicating."

She didn't respond.

His fingers touched her collarbone, tracing it like a signature. "Are you afraid of me, Charlotte?"

She met his eyes. "Should I be?"

Philippe smiled and reclined. "No. But you should understand me."

She stayed still, heartbeat loud. The air in the room felt heavier now.

"I don't want just beauty," he said. "I want sincerity. Emotion. Submission with spirit. You have spirit."

She nodded, the room swimming slightly.

"You will stay with me tonight," he said, not asking.

She didn't answer. But she didn't stand either. The waves broke against the cliffs. The night closed in around them.

The hallway to Philippe's bedroom was silent, save for the low hum of distant waves and her own pulse. The house seemed to shift its tone as the night deepened, no longer a paradise, but a stage set for something private, primal, and negotiated in invisible ink.

The doors were already open.

The room was vast. Too vast. No pictures, no mess, no softness, just a sprawling bed with sheets turned down, dim gold lamps glowing like sentinels. A decanter of water sat beside a glass. One robe, folded at the edge. A single black suit jacket, discarded on a chaise.

He was in the bathroom, whistling.

Charlotte moved to the balcony first. She stepped out and breathed in the Mediterranean night. The sky was deep ink, and the sea below murmured secrets in the dark. Somewhere far off, a yacht's lights blinked against the horizon.

She wanted to be on that yacht, drifting far from here. Far from the silk robe she now slipped over her lingerie. Far from the voice that echoed from the bathroom, his voice, charming and precise.

She didn't belong to this life. Not really. Not yet.

"Come inside, ma belle."

His voice was gentle, but the command under it was clear.

She turned, closing the glass doors behind her.

He was standing in a towel, his chest smooth, his stomach soft. He held a bottle of lotion, anointing his hands like a ritual. Charlotte stood by the bed, still, expression unreadable.

"Sit," he said.

She sat.

He moved behind her and began to rub the lotion into her shoulders. His hands were too practiced. The touch wasn't meant to relax, it was a transaction.

"You're tense," he murmured.

She said nothing.

"I don't want to break you," he continued, his lips close to her ear. "I want to see you."

He leaned down and kissed her shoulder.

She flinched.

He paused, just for a second. "Ah," he whispered. "There it is."

Charlotte closed her eyes. In that moment, everything blurred: the club, the drugs, the men, the mirror in her New York apartment with lipstick kisses smeared across its face. The way Dylan had touched her wrist once in the dressing room. The smell of bleach and roses. Her brother's voice when she was eleven.

"You're somewhere else," Philippe said. "Come back."

But she couldn't. Her mind split, and it always split the same way: one part present, the other one - a little girl from a small town.

She stood.

Philippe didn't stop her. He only watched.

"I need a minute," she said, walking to the bathroom. She locked the door behind her and leaned on the sink, gripping porcelain like a ledge.

The face that looked back in the mirror was flawless, but her eyes betrayed her. Too wide. Too full of things she hadn't said.

This is just a role, she told herself. You're good at roles.

She splashed water on her face. Counted to ten. Swallowed the fear and walked back into the bedroom.

Philippe was already in bed, covers drawn back. He reached for her.

She let him.

But her body was far away - coastal, ghosted, a performance rehearsed into muscle memory. He liked to whisper things. She hated the way he called her "little flame." It reminded her of the night with Victor. The time in the VIP room. The way her own shame had become currency.

Afterward, he fell asleep easily. Snoring gently, like a man who knew the world was his.

She lay beside him, staring at the ceiling.

A single tear slid down her cheek, disappearing into the white silk pillow.

The first thing she noticed was how quiet it was. Charlotte opened her eyes slowly. The room was washed in silver, light pressing through gauzy curtains. Philippe's house was all minimalism and control - a museum of wealth where nothing was left to chance. She lay there on smooth, cold sheets that didn't feel slept in. Only her side of the bed was messy.

Philippe was gone.

Her body ached in a way that wasn't exactly painful but wasn't right either. Her mind flashed with blurred images from the night before: champagne, that too-perfect laugh, his fingers on her wrist, not quite tight but definite. She remembered the mirror above the bed and the way he'd watched her, not with desire, but with curiosity. Like a collector admiring something rare before locking it away.

Her heart knocked once, hard, but she stayed still, listening. No voices. No footsteps. Only the hum of the city below, muffled by glass and wealth. She wrapped the white sheet around her and padded barefoot across the marble floor. The living room was immaculate. A decanter of whiskey. A long, modern sofa. A thin laptop resting open on the table.

She hesitated, then stepped closer.

The glow from the screen was the only light in the room, casting a cold bluish hue across Philippe's desk. It wasn't locked. That alone made her uneasy, as if he wanted her to see.

Rows of spreadsheets were open, layered like strata in some corporate excavation site.

Tab 1:
"Viability Report - Q2"

Charlotte's eyes scanned the columns.
Names. Ages. Blood types. Genetic profiles. Substance use history. Last known physical evaluations.
Each row was color-coded - Green: Prime Viable. Yellow: Degrading. Red: Expired.

Next to some names were notes:

"Pregnant - 2nd trimester. Potential for dual extraction."
"Previous cesarean - scar tissue noted."
"Scheduled for retirement 07/06. Heart flagged for transplant matching Tier I."

She clicked into a dropdown. A list of tags appeared:

Escort - Premium
Escort - Aged Out
Incubator
Organ Reserve

It wasn't a business. It was a system. A pipeline.
Polished and precise.
Her stomach turned.
She moved to the next tab.

Tab 2:
"Client Screening - Tier I Organ Buyers"

It was worse.
Private clients. Most with titles: Lord, Sheikh, Ambassador, CEO.
Each buyer had their own profile, complete with preferences - age of donor, organ preferences,

"purity" status, willingness to fund surrogate cycles.

Next to each name was a tally: # of purchases made.

Some were in double digits.

Photos.

Girls. Some she recognized from parties. From the club. From Philippe's side. All marked with status notes: out of commission, health declined, sold.

One file caught her eye:

"Custom Request: Arthur - Priority heart match confirmed. Stage 3 incubation viable. Last cycle: 6 weeks ago. Scheduled for retrieval asap."

Status: Pending retrieval.

She stopped breathing.

"Pending retrieval."

Charlotte's hands trembled as she backed away from the screen.

This wasn't an escort ring.

It was industrialized body theft.

They didn't just sell the girls for pleasure - they used them up.

As luxury wombs. As organ stock. As disposable property.

That's why no one ever really left.

The screen flickered.

And behind her, a floorboard creaked.

Charlotte felt her throat close. Her vision blurred and tunneled.

A small noise - a door. She spun around.

Philippe stood in the hallway, smiling casually, a mug of coffee in his hand like it was any other morning. "You're up early," he said. "Sleep well?"

Charlotte's mouth was dry. She forced herself to nod.

He walked toward her slowly, eyes glinting with something unreadable. "Did you go snooping?"

She shook her head. "No."

He was close now. Too close. He reached out and brushed a strand of hair behind her ear, his touch feather-light. "Good," he said, voice smooth. "Because curiosity can be… dangerous in our world."

Then he kissed her forehead like a father. Like a priest. Like death.

She didn't say another word.

Philippe turned his back to her and walked toward the kitchen, humming something low and French under his breath. She took that moment - her one chance - and slipped down the hallway, grabbed her heels from where they'd been kicked off by the mirror last night, and slid into them with numb fingers. Her dress was crumpled on the floor, still damp with perfume and sweat. She didn't bother with her bra.

She moved like she was underwater. Like a dreamer trying to wake up.

The hallway walk was silent. Polished chrome, bright lights, her own reflection - a ghost with smudged mascara and hollow eyes. Her heartbeat didn't slow until she was outside on the street, where the air tasted like fog and car exhaust, and real life pressed against her skin again.

But even out here, she felt watched.

Philippe's world didn't stop at his front door. He had people. Eyes. Shadows in black cars and glass towers. And now she knew too much.

Charlotte turned down a side street and kept walking. Fast. Heels clicking. Her breath growing shallow. She felt like she might throw up but didn't want to stop.

She tried to piece it all together. The whispers at parties. The way some of the girls just disappeared. The way Lilly had stopped answering her texts some nights, then showed up with new jewelry and hollow laughter. The "exclusive clients." The long trips to places no one ever talked about.

Retired Assets.

Organ buyers.

It was slaughter.

She stumbled into a coffee shop and sat at the back, hands trembling as she typed Lilly's name into her phone. Still no response. She sent a message:

"Lilly. Call me. Now. It's serious. It's about Philippe."

Charlotte stared at the screen, willing it to buzz, to ring, to bring her something solid to hold onto.

But it stayed dark.

When the waitress came by to ask if she wanted anything, Charlotte just shook her head.

She didn't want anything. Not coffee. Not sleep. Not sex. Not diamonds.

She just wanted out.

Chapter 16: The Chase

Charlotte found Lilly in a hotel suite, curled up in bed with silk sheets wrapped around her like a cocoon. The curtains were drawn tight, the room lit only by the blue haze of the TV screen playing something no one was watching. Empty champagne flutes glittered on the table, and the sharp tang of last night's perfume still clung to the air.

"Lilly."

Lilly blinked awake, dazed, mascara crusted beneath her lashes. "What are you doing"

"He's selling girls," Charlotte said, stepping inside and locking the door behind her. "Organs. That's what happens when they disappear. They don't get out. He sells them."

Lilly sat up slowly. "What the fuck are you talking about?"

"I saw it. On his laptop. Folders. Names. Pictures. Notes about whose bodies are still 'viable' Lilly, he has a folder called Retired Assets."

Lilly was silent. Her mouth opened, then closed again.

"You knew." Charlotte's voice cracked. "Jesus Christ, you knew."

"I didn't" Lilly's eyes flicked toward the window. "I didn't want to know."

"But you did," Charlotte whispered.

Silence. The kind that fills a room like gas before the spark.

"I found a file," she said finally, her voice thin and breaking at the edges.

Lilly stopped.

"What file?"

Charlotte laughed once, bitter and small.

"Don't pretend."

"It had my name on it."

Lilly's throat tightened.

"It said: Priority heart match confirmed. Stage 3 incubation viable. Scheduled for retrieval asap."

Lilly didn't answer.

"A brand-new heart for Arthur."

Her hands began to shake.

"I thought it was some mistake at first. A wrong file. But then I looked closer... and it had everything. My blood type. My surgery history. The implants. Even that thing on my back I had removed when I was a teenager."

She took a breath. It felt like drowning.

"I'm not a person in their system. I'm an organ. A product. Just waiting to be cracked open."

Lilly turned away... "I thought I could protect you."

Charlotte laughed again, louder now. "By leaving me alone with him? By letting them plan my retrieval like I'm a fucking cow led to slaughter?"

Lilly's eyes filled. "I didn't know it would be you."

Charlotte's face fell. The last drop of trust drained out of her.

Lilly moved - throwing off the sheets, scrambling for her phone, her bag. "We need to go. We need to go now."

"He never lets them go. The girls who tried…" Lilly's voice trailed off. "They vanish. Their names get wiped. There was a Ukrainian girl - Nadiya - she broke contract, tried to run. Three days later, Philippe sent me a necklace she used to wear. Said I'd earned it."

Charlotte's stomach turned. "You stayed?"

Lilly looked at her. "Do you think I had a choice?"

They packed fast. No makeup. No heels. Just IDs, cash, burner phones. Charlotte left her designer bag behind. It felt radioactive now, one more thread tied to Philippe's world.

When they hit the lobby, it was crawling with men in dark suits. One at the desk. Another by the elevator. A third pretending to read a newspaper, eyes flicking over the top as they passed.

Lilly didn't look up. She grabbed Charlotte's hand and whispered, "Back entrance."

They slipped through the hotel kitchen, white tile, steam, knives clattering. A dishwasher cursed in Portuguese as they brushed past him. The back door was unmarked, but Lilly knew the path. She'd done this before.

They stepped into the alley. Cold, wet. The city breathing in shadows.

Then a voice, low, in French, crackled behind them. "Stop them."

Lilly ran. Charlotte followed.

Their heels slapped the pavement as they bolted down the alley and into the street, weaving between cars, dodging horns and shouting pedestrians. Charlotte's lungs burned. Lilly's bag flew open, lipsticks and notes and a roll of cash scattering like confetti.

They didn't stop.

Around the corner, through a construction site, over scaffolding and wet boards. A man in a black coat started chasing, fast, deliberate, trained.

Charlotte's shoe snapped. She kicked it off and kept going barefoot. Blood bloomed where her foot struck glass, but she didn't feel it. Not yet.

"We can't go to the police," Lilly gasped as they ducked into a tube station. "He owns them."

Charlotte wanted to scream. "Then where?"

Lilly pointed to the west. "There's a safe house. It's run by a woman named Sofya. She used to work for him. She got out. But we have to be careful. There are eyes everywhere."

They ran breathless, shivering. The streets were nearly empty. When two men in suits caught up with them.

Lilly's eyes locked on Charlotte's. They didn't speak.

One of the men reached for Charlotte's arm, she twisted free, elbowed him in the gut, kept running.

Around a corner. Past a church, through a cemetery gate.

They crouched behind a stone angel, panting, hearts like trapped birds.

Lilly's mascara streaked her cheeks. "This is what hell feels like," she whispered.

Charlotte wanted to cry. Or vomit. Or scream into the sky. But all she did was grab Lilly's hand again and say, "We're getting out. I don't care if I have to tear the whole world down. We're getting out."

A phone buzzed.

Charlotte froze. It wasn't hers.

Lilly pulled out her burner. One message: "You're making this difficult. Come back now. You'll only make it worse." - P

Lilly dropped the phone like it was on fire. It hit the gravel and cracked.

Charlotte crushed it under her heel.

Somewhere behind them, tires screeched. Dogs barked. The wind shifted.

"They found us," Charlotte whispered.

They ran again.

Through back alleys and bus depots. Across bridges. No taxis would stop for them - not barefoot, not bleeding, not with terror stamped across their faces. Charlotte saw herself in a darkened window, wild-eyed, shaking, not a girl anymore. Not even a woman.

A hunted thing.

They finally reached the address Lilly had whispered through chattering teeth - a red door behind a bookstore. No bell. No sign. Just a symbol scratched into the wood, a crescent and a line.

Charlotte knocked. Nothing.

Again. Harder.

Footsteps. A bolt sliding back.

The door opened an inch. A woman's eyes stared out - dark, sharp, wary.

Lilly whispered, "Sofya sent me once. Please. Philippe's after us."

The door opened.

They stumbled inside. The smell of sage and dust hit them first. Then the warmth. Then silence.

The woman who let them in was older. Maybe forty. Hair tied back, face lined with worry or wisdom, Charlotte couldn't tell.

"You've got blood on your foot," she said to Charlotte, nodding toward the couch. "Sit. I'll get something for it."

Charlotte collapsed.

Lilly paced the room like an animal in a cage.

"You understand what you've done?" the woman asked as she returned with gauze and peroxide.

"We ran," Charlotte said.

"No." The woman shook her head. "You broke the circle. Girls don't run. Not from Philippe. Not from them. You didn't just run from a man, you ran from a network. A machine."

Charlotte looked up. "Then what happens now?"

The woman smiled faintly. "Now you find out if you're fast enough."

The woman stitched Charlotte's foot without asking too many questions. She moved like someone who'd done this before - clean, efficient, silent. Her name, they learned, was Sasha. She didn't smile often, and when she did, it looked like it hurt.

"You'll want to stay in the back room," she said, finishing the last knot and taping gauze over it. "There are no windows. Less chance of being spotted. We burn the phones in the morning. After that, no contact. No social media. No clubs. No old clients. You disappear. That's how this works."

Lilly sank into a worn armchair. "What happens if we don't?"

Sasha didn't answer. Just looked at her and in that silence was a hundred stories. All of them bad.

Charlotte leaned back against the wall, heart still stuttering. The room was dim and smelled faintly of incense and books. Wind whispered through the old windowpanes. Somewhere beneath it all was the city: alive, uncaring.

"Do you think he knows where we are?"
Charlotte asked.

Lilly didn't respond. She was staring at the floor,
knees drawn up, arms crossed over her chest like
a child trying to hold herself together.

Charlotte pressed. "Lilly?"

She flinched. "He always knows. But maybe he'll
wait. Maybe he'll think it's not worth it this
time."

Charlotte wanted to believe that. She needed to
believe that. But the image of Philippe's smile -
that slow, knowing curve, wouldn't leave her.

"He's not the kind of man who lets things go,"
Charlotte whispered.

Sasha poured tea in silence. The clock ticked on
the wall. The power buzzed in the floorboards.

Outside, a car passed.

Then another.

Then nothing.

Just stillness. And breath. And fear.

Charlotte's mind spun with memory. Philippe's
place. The taste of expensive wine. The folder
marked Assets. The way he'd touched her
shoulder like she already belonged to him.

How long had she been walking into a trap?

How long had Lilly known?

And now what?

She didn't know who to be anymore. Her beauty
had once been armor. Now it felt like bait.

The clock ticked.

11:07 p.m.

She turned to Sasha. "Why do you help girls like us?"

Sasha looked up. Her eyes were bottomless. "Because no one helped me."

She said nothing else.

Somewhere outside, a dog barked. Tires screeched. Then silence again.

Too much silence.

Charlotte moved to the window, careful not to disturb the curtain. She peeked through a sliver.

A black car sat across the street. Lights off. Engine running.

She stepped back.

"They found us," she said.

Lilly bolted upright. "How? We…"

"Because they always do," Sasha interrupted. "And because Philippe doesn't send amateurs. We have three exits. The tunnel beneath the bookshop leads to the next street. You go when I say, not a moment before. Understand?"

Charlotte nodded, pulse pounding.

Sasha extinguished the candles. Darkness dropped like a curtain. Then the sound of footsteps outside.

Boots. Heavy. Purposeful.

Three knocks at the front door. Slow. Measured. Confident.

Charlotte held her breath.

Another knock. Then silence.

Then a voice, muffled, accented, polite. "We're looking for two women. Runaways. We have reason to believe they're in this building."

Charlotte squeezed Lilly's hand. Sasha didn't move.

The voice continued. "You're harboring property, madam. That's a crime."

The word property landed like a blade.

Sasha moved to a panel in the floor, pulled it up without a sound, and gestured toward the dark space beneath.

"Go," she mouthed.

Charlotte didn't think. She just pulled Lilly down into the darkness, into the tunnel, into the unknown.

Above them, another knock.

Then wood splintering.

Then chaos.

Philippe.

The room was cold, despite the fire flickering in the hearth. Philippe liked it that way, the contrast between warmth and control. He sat in a leather chair, legs crossed, a glass of Chateauneuf du pape in his hand. The security feed flickered silently on the monitor before him. Grainy black-and-white footage of the bookstore safe house. A man's voice crackled in through the speaker. "They were here, sir. The healer helped them escape. We're sweeping the tunnels now."

Philippe sighed and set the glass down on the mahogany table. "She always was sentimental." He touched a button and the screen split into four. Footage from his properties. One from the medical wing. Another from the birthing suite. A third from the spa where the younger girls trained. The fourth… an organ bank, pristine and humming, rows of surgical beds lit in sterile white.

There was no blood in sight. Just potential.

"Find the girls," he said calmly. "I want them back alive. Especially the blonde."

Charlotte.

He leaned back and laced his fingers. The beautiful ones always thought they were the exception. They thought their charm could outlast the system.

They were wrong.

This wasn't just about escorting, that was the surface. The silk wrapping around the meat.

The real business was longevity. Wealth preservation. Life as a commodity.

First, the girls were trained. Poised, seductive, flawless. Rented by billionaires and royalty who paid not just for pleasure, but for secrecy, for power. Ten thousand pounds an hour. Sometimes more. Their value was high at the start.

But beauty fades. Even with surgeries and discipline, they aged. After a few years, clients lost interest. That's when Stage Two began.

Philippe had perfected it: The Incubator Program. Elite clients: oligarchs, oil magnates, dynastic heirs - many of them couldn't have children. Or their wives refused. Or they wanted bloodlines clean of scandal. Philippe offered something better than surrogates: silence, total control, and a perfect genetic profile.

The girls were reassigned, paired discreetly with chosen donors. Their bodies monitored; their wombs contracted out under binding agreements. No one asked questions. No one dared.

The girls never knew the full truth. Some were told it was a medical detox, a recovery program. Others were told it was part of their retirement package. By the time they realized what was happening, it was too late.

After birth, they were sent to the final phase. The Harvest.

Philippe didn't like the word. Too pastoral. But it fit.

Organs were lucrative. Especially hearts, livers, kidneys from healthy young women who had lived in a carefully monitored environment. No drugs after a certain age. No infections.

Everything preserved for the final transaction. Each body yielded hundreds of thousands, sometimes millions.

Some of the organs went to discreet private hospitals.

Others to clients with standing contracts - the ones who believed money should conquer death.

The rest?

Well. Nothing went to waste.

Philippe stood and adjusted his cufflinks. The silk glinted under the chandelier.

Charlotte had potential. He had handpicked her.

But now she was running.

He smiled faintly.

They always ran.

And they always came back: broken, desperate, or dead.

The tunnel pressed in around them like a throat.

It stank of earth and rot and old water.

Somewhere above, Charlotte could still hear faint sounds, the thud of boots, a shout, maybe a door being ripped from its hinges. Then quiet again.

Like something had shifted to listening mode.

Lilly gripped Charlotte's wrist so tightly it hurt.

"How long is this tunnel?" Charlotte whispered; voice barely audible over their own breathing.

"I don't know," Lilly rasped. "Sasha said it leads to the next street. But what if they're waiting there too?"

Charlotte kept moving, hunched, her injured foot throbbing. Her bandage was soaked, but she couldn't stop. The walls were wet with condensation, and the floor dipped in slick places. She could barely see.

It wasn't just the dark that terrified her.

It was the silence.

The kind of silence where you know someone is listening on the other side of it.

Every sound she made, every scuff of a shoe, every breath felt like it echoed for miles. She half-expected Philippe's voice to come through the tunnel walls like some twisted god: You didn't really think you could leave, did you?

A loud clang behind them.

They both froze.

Then a shout.

"They're in the tunnel!"

Lilly's face drained of color. Charlotte grabbed her arm.

"Run," she breathed. "Run, now."

They bolted forward, slipping and stumbling in the half-dark. The tunnel forked suddenly - left or right.

Charlotte hesitated. "Which way?!"

"I don't know!"

Behind them - the sound of boots slapping wet stone. Flashlight beams flickering in the dark.

Charlotte chose right.

She ducked into the smaller passage, nearly crawling now, heart battering against her ribs like it wanted out. The air grew tighter. The walls narrowed. The smell was worse here: sewage, maybe. Blood.

The tunnel turned hard left.

Then stairs.

Up.

Lilly reached them first, shoving open a rusted grate with both hands. It groaned loud, so loud, and Charlotte prayed no one had heard it. They scrambled up into a shadowed alley between two buildings. Night air hit them like a slap.

But there was no relief.

Just more shadows.

They started running again, limping and gasping, half-dragging each other through the city's veins. Behind them: the clatter of a metal gate. Voices. Philippe's men.

"Split up," Charlotte gasped.

"No!"

"We'll lead them in different directions, they can't follow both of us. Just meet me at the airport. Noon tomorrow. Under the arrivals sign."

Lilly hesitated; eyes wide with panic.

"Promise me," Charlotte begged.

Lilly nodded, tears streaking her face. "Promise."

They parted without a hug. There was no time for soft things.

Charlotte ducked into an alley, climbing a rusted fire escape with her good foot. Her hands shook as she pulled herself higher, hiding behind trash bins and vents as the footsteps passed below her. Don't look down. Don't cry. Don't break.

Somewhere behind her, a man's voice barked into a phone: "I saw the tall one! She went east."

They were triangulating them.

Charlotte's head spun.

The city wasn't a refuge. It was a cage. And Philippe had the keys to all its locks.

Charlotte's breath fogged in the cold night as she slipped from one shadow to the next, her footsteps light but frantic. Every face on the street was a potential threat; every glance could be a tracker's signal. The city had transformed into a sprawling maze of predators.

She avoided the main roads, sticking to narrow alleyways where the glow of street lamps barely reached. The ache in her foot throbbed steadily, each step a reminder of how vulnerable she was. Her phone was dead. No contacts. No way to call Lilly. No way to know if Lilly was alive.

Her stomach clenched with hunger and panic. She pushed forward, desperate to find shelter before dawn.

Hours later, she found herself crouched behind a dumpster in a shadowed courtyard. The distant hum of traffic was muffled, but never far. She pulled her jacket tighter around her thin frame, shivering in the chill.

A group of homeless people gathered near a warming fire a few feet away. Their wary eyes flicked to her, but no one approached. Charlotte debated moving on, but exhaustion clawed at her limbs.

Quietly, she edged toward the fire and mumbled, "Please… just for a little while."

A grizzled man with a crooked smile nodded and handed her a worn blanket. The warmth seeped through the fabric, but the cold inside her didn't budge.

She listened to the murmur of voices, stories of loss, addiction, survival and realized she was no different from them now. Just another ghost in the city.

Sleep came fitfully, haunted by nightmares of Philippe's cold eyes, the gleaming surgical rooms, and Lilly's terrified face.

At dawn, she moved again, slipping like a shadow. The crowds were thicker now - the perfect cover, but her eyes scanned constantly for anyone in black suits or radios.

At one point, a man brushed past her too deliberately, his hand in his coat pocket.

Charlotte's heart froze.

She broke into a run.

"Stop her!" a voice barked.

Panting, limping, she scrambled out into the open street, adrenaline fueling her.

The chase was far from over.

Chapter 17: The Skin Trade

The city was a blur.

Charlotte hadn't slept in two nights. Her body had begun to separate from itself, her limbs moved but felt foreign, her thoughts drifted in broken spirals. Time no longer came in hours, but in gut-tightening moments. A glance over her shoulder. A man's hand in his pocket. A security camera on a street lamp.

She was becoming invisible.

Or maybe she was just slipping out of her own skin.

Airport loomed ahead like a beast. Grand, indifferent. She moved through it carefully, scanning faces, searching for red hair. Lilly wasn't there.

She checked the clock again: 12:04.

Charlotte clung to the steel beam beside the arrivals sign. Her breath was shallow. The pain in her foot had grown sharper, a throbbing, infected pulse. She wanted to sit, but she didn't trust the stillness.

Every instinct screamed that something was wrong.

And then it happened.

She caught the movement too late, a figure closing in fast from her right. Another flanking from the left. She tried to bolt, but hands were

already on her. Not rough at first - practiced.
Hands that knew how to restrain without making
a scene. Hands that had done this before.
"Don't make this harder," one of them said
quietly.
Charlotte screamed anyway.
The sound cut through like a gunshot, but no one
helped. A businessman turned his head. A woman
slowed but didn't stop. The men moved fast
through a side door, down a hall, into the
underground car park.
Then silence.
She was shoved into the back of a black SUV,
arms pinned behind her. The doors locked. The
air inside smelled like leather and something
sweet - a cologne she'd smelled once before. On
Philippe.
Tears blurred her vision.
She didn't ask where they were taking her.
She already knew.

The SUV's interior was silent, save for the hum
of tires on wet asphalt. Charlotte sat between two
of Philippe's men, her wrists zip-tied behind her.
Her cheek was pressed to the cold window.
Outside, Nice blurred, gray skies, blinking traffic
lights, faces she'd never see again.
Her voice was gone from screaming.
The man on her right, square-jawed with a
trimmed beard, looked at her like she wasn't a

person anymore. Not a threat. Not a victim. Just an object in transit.

She forced herself to stay still. Panic would only make it worse.

They crossed a bridge and turned toward the body of water, toward the part of the city where men like Philippe built private fortresses behind wrought iron gates. She recognized the route. Her stomach knotted with every passing block. The villas came into view - Philippe's penthouse wrapped in tinted glass and cold luxury.

When the car stopped, no one spoke.

The bearded man stepped out first, then pulled her with him.

Charlotte stumbled. Her knees gave out.

He didn't bother to help her up. Just dragged her across the pavement.

They entered through the garage, all polished stone and dim blue lights, then into a private elevator with mirrored walls. She couldn't look at her reflection. The bruises on her throat, the dirt under her nails. Her hair in knots. Her eyes empty.

The doors opened.

A hallway of black marble stretched ahead. The guards didn't guide her this time, they shoved her forward like a dog returned to its master.

She moved slowly.

Her footsteps echoed against the walls.

And then she saw him.

Philippe stood at the end of the corridor; hands folded behind his back. A figure carved from ice. He wore a dark silk shirt, unbuttoned at the collar, and black slacks that flowed like liquid shadow. His eyes met hers, and they didn't blink.

"You've disappointed me, Charlotte," he said, his voice low and clinical. "I gave you the world."

She stopped ten feet from him. Her wrists still bound. Her jaw clenched.

"You gave me a cage."

He smiled, a sharp, unsettling curve.

"Ungrateful girls always find their way back. Sooner or later. We own more than you realize."

He stepped forward and took her chin between his fingers. She flinched.

He didn't let go.

"Your fear used to be... delicious," he murmured. "But now, it's become tedious."

Behind her, the elevator doors slid shut.

She was completely alone with him now.

"Let me go," she said. Her voice cracked.

Philippe leaned in, his breath brushing her skin.

"Let you go? No, angel. You don't leave this world. You get used. Or you get erased."

Then he struck her open palm, across the face.

Not rage. Not emotion.

Just method.

Like resetting a puppet.

Charlotte's head snapped sideways from the force. Her vision exploded into sparks. Blood filled her mouth where her cheek split open against her molars.

She didn't cry out.

Philippe stepped back and wiped his hand casually on a black silk handkerchief, as if brushing off lint.

"I don't enjoy doing that," he said flatly, "but sometimes softness breeds stupidity."

She spat blood at his feet.

He looked at it, then at her, unimpressed.

"You always had spirit. That's why I picked you."

Charlotte's knees buckled, but she remained upright. "Picked me for what?"

Philippe gave a faint laugh - one without joy.

"You still think this is about sex, don't you?" He gestured for one of the guards to approach. "Take her downstairs. Show her what comes next."

"No" she started, but a sharp blow to the back of her legs took her down.

They dragged her through a side hallway, past velvet curtains and mirrored walls, to a steel door embedded with biometric scanners. The space beyond smelled of antiseptic and concrete.

Below the penthouse, Philippe kept another world.

A world of metal beds and silent cameras. A world where women no longer had names - just files. Charlotte saw girls strapped to gurneys, some sleeping, some sedated. Some - too quiet to be asleep, stared at the ceiling with eyes that no longer registered light.

She screamed then. Fought until her wrists bled against the zip ties. But no one heard her over the hiss of machines and the hum of generators.

"This is where the contract ends," Philippe's voice came through.

He turned and looked her dead in the eyes.

"Everything has a market, Charlotte. And you…you are very… marketable."

She wanted to collapse. She wanted to die. But her body refused. Something inside her, animal, primal, kept her upright.

They shoved her into a glass-walled holding room. Clean. White. Sterile.

The door locked behind her.

She was alone.

For now.

The glass chamber was cold and silent. A white cot, a metal toilet, and a sink were the only furnishings. Charlotte sat with her knees pulled to her chest, staring at the ceiling. Her heartbeat was a drumbeat of panic in her throat.

No sound came from the corridor. No footsteps. No voices.

Time dissolved.

Her lip had stopped bleeding. Her wrists were raw. Her body ached, but it was the dull ache of something that no longer expected rescue.

Then - a whisper.

Faint, almost imagined.

She sat up.

Another whisper, closer this time. It came from the vent near the ceiling. A slit in the wall, barely visible.

Charlotte stood on the cot and pressed her ear to the vent.

"Can you hear me?" The voice was female. Young. Urgent.

"Yes," she whispered back. "Who are you?"

A pause. Then: "I'm called Evie. I work in the surgical unit."

Charlotte's throat tightened. "Please. Help me. I can't stay here."

Evie's breath hitched. "You weren't supposed to come back. You ran. Most girls who run… they don't make it this far."

Charlotte swallowed hard. "Why are you talking to me?"

Another pause.

"Because I was one of you. Before I put on the mask."

Charlotte slid to the floor, trembling.

Evie spoke quickly now, like she was racing a clock. "There's a waste chute two levels down

through the utility shaft. No cameras. But you'll need a keycard. I can hide one in your food tray."
Charlotte's pulse soared. "Thank you. Thank you" Evie's voice cut off.
Footsteps outside. Charlotte scrambled away from the vent.
A man in a white coat appeared at the glass wall. Philippe's head surgeon. His smile was professional, practiced.
"Miss?" he said, tapping the glass. "It's time for your screening."
The door opened.
Two guards entered. One held a syringe.
Charlotte tried to fight, but the needle slid in before she could scream. The world pitched sideways. Cold flooded her veins. Her limbs turned to wax.
The last thing she saw was Philippe's reflection in the glass, watching her from the shadows.

Chapter 18: The Exit

The rain burned her eyes.

Charlotte staggered through the alley behind the clinic, barefoot, soaked, half-dressed in surgical scrubs. Her skin was mottled with track marks and bruises. One eye swollen shut. A stitch in her side from where they'd started cutting. She didn't remember getting out, just Evie's voice in her ear, her arms under Charlotte's shoulders, the blur of hallways, a lift, cold wind, open sky.

"You have ten minutes before they trace the breach," Evie had said. "Run. Don't turn around." Now it was night.
Charlotte pushed her body forward, block by block, weaving through garbage bins and shuttered shops. The city pulsed around her, unaware. She could hear herself breathing like a dying animal. But she was free.
She didn't know where she was.
Somewhere near the docks. Wet concrete and broken neon. She ducked into a stairwell beside a pub and collapsed against the wall.
Her hand reached inside her pocket, Evie had tucked something there. A flash drive. Red plastic. Cold as bone. A digital ledger, Evie had said. Names. Procedures. Clients. Evidence.

"Get this to someone who can bury him," she'd whispered.

Charlotte stared at it.

Then she vomited beside it.

The sky split with thunder.

Somewhere across the street, a man in a black coat turned his head.

She saw him.

And ran.

Charlotte reached the safe-house by dawn. It was a narrow flat above a corner bookshop, gray and silent. The door was ajar, just like Evie said it would be.

Inside: warmth. A kettle steaming. Clean clothes folded on a chair. A woman stood near the window - older, in her fifties, with silver-streaked hair pulled back and wire-rimmed glasses. Her name was Mara. Evie had trusted her.

"You're Charlotte?" the woman asked, voice low. Charlotte nodded. Her lips were cracked and bleeding. Her legs gave out. Mara caught her gently.

"Sit," she said. "You're safe now."

Hot tea. A bath. A bed with real sheets. For the first time in days, Charlotte cried. Not from fear, but from the sudden illusion of peace.

She handed Mara the flash drive. "Evie said you'd know what to do with this."

Mara turned it over in her fingers. Her expression unreadable. "We've been waiting for this. You did the right thing."

Charlotte's eyes closed. Exhaustion swallowed her.

She didn't see Mara lock the door behind her.

Didn't hear her whisper into the burner phone.

Just the hush of water pipes, the creak of stairs, and the distant hum of Nice.

When she woke, the room was darker.

And she wasn't alone.

Philippe sat at the desk beside the bed, sipping from her cup of tea.

Her scream caught in her throat.

Mara stood behind him, arms crossed.

"I told you she'd come," she said.

Philippe set the cup down carefully.

Charlotte tried to stand. Her legs didn't work. Her vision swam.

Mara had drugged the tea.

Philippe rose.

"Do you know what I do to broken things, Charlotte?"

He bent to her ear.

"I recycle them."

She didn't remember the next hour - only pain. A hallway. Needles. Straps. The sterile smell again. But this time, there would be no Evie to help her escape.

It was white.

White light. White ceiling. White sheets.

Charlotte floated. At least that's how it felt. As though her body had been left behind somewhere and what remained was a ghost inside her skull.

She tried to speak.

No voice came.

She tried to move.

Strapped. Arms. Legs. Chest.

A tube down her throat.

Beeping nearby.

A surgeon's masked face hovered over her. Then another. Then two more. She couldn't tell them apart. It was as if they were multiplying, duplicating like cells under a microscope.

They didn't see her. They saw it. The body.

She heard them speaking.

"Liver's strong. Kidneys too. We need the Heart, it's borderline - damage from withdrawal, but viable."

A pause.

"She's a priority tissue."

Laughter, clinical and cold.

Charlotte screamed inside her mind.

No sound.

This isn't real. This isn't real.

But it was.

She saw a flash of Evie's face. A memory, soft and warm. The hallway. The lift. The night air.

Then another face - Lilly, back at the beginning. In glitter. Laughing in a bathroom stall. "You're not meant for normal, baby. You're meant for fire."

More faces.

Maria. Valery. Dylan. Her mother. The dog she had as a child. Her first kiss.

It all blurred into color.

A flood of memory and scent and sound.

Take it all, she thought. Take the body. I was never just that anyway.

The blade entered. She didn't feel it. Her mind had already stepped out of the room.

Above her, the white light cracked open, like the skin of an egg and through it, she saw sky.

Not Nice or London sky. Not now.

But her own. The one from home. Wide. Open. Blue.

She walked toward it.

Barefoot. Free.

Epilogue: The Afterlife

Long after her body was erased, the stories emerged.

Some said she went to Paris.

Others whispered she married rich and never looked back.

There were rumors she was spotted on a yacht in Nice, champagne in hand, laughing like she'd never bled. A ghost in gold heels, untouched by time.

The club girls remembered her in fragments: the way she moved, the laugh that cut through bass, the storm in her eyes. Valery once said she danced like she was escaping something no one could see.

Rob kept her photo in his office drawer. He never told anyone why.

And Dylan... well, he never spoke her name again. But sometimes, when the lights hit just right and the right song played, he'd stare out over the VIP floor like he saw someone who wasn't there.

She was the girl with glitter in her veins and fire on her heels.

The one who lived too fast, too hard, too beautifully.

And for a moment, even if just a flicker, she had it all. Money. Power. Worship.

Not the kind that lasts.

But the kind that burns.

The kind that makes people say, "Do you remember her?"

And maybe, just maybe, someone does.

A story that cut deep and heal slowly.